LANDSCAPING LOVE

Quinn Valley Ranch, Book 3

LIZ ISAACSON

ISBN-13: 978-1638761259

CHAPTER ONE

*C*apri Haywood sucked in a breath, her eyes taking in the dilapidated condition of the house.

"See how the wood's rotted here?"

She saw it, and she nodded at the man who'd met her to let her in the house. It was only a rental, but it was also the only place Capri had to stay that night. Her emotions choked her, making breathing difficult.

"Ma'am, do you have somewhere else you can stay?" he asked.

She shook her head, tight little bursts of movement that felt like they'd crack her neck. Splinter her spine.

"I can't believe Parker thought he could rent this place," Gerald said, shaking his head. "There's not even carpet on the floor."

Capri let her eyes sweep over the concrete before she turned away. Quinn Valley was turning out to be as bad as Crescent Lake.

No, she told herself as she went down the front steps. Nothing would be as bad as staying in Crescent Lake.

"Is there a hotel?" she managed to ask, her voice so unlike her own.

"Sure thing." Gerald looked at the truck and trailer Capri had pulled all the way from Texas. Exhaustion ran through her at the thought of trying to park the outfit somewhere in town. Maybe she could leave it here. Grab her suitcase from the back and have Gerald take her to the hotel.

He was an older gentleman, probably in his late fifties, and he lived just down the road from the house. "The Quinn Hotel and Spa," he said. "Best in town, and it's close to everything."

"Probably not the ranch," she said, looking at Gerald out of the corner of her eye. "Right?"

"Oh, no, not the ranch," he said, shaking his head. "That's north of here. Twenty minutes or so. Can't miss it."

Capri was sure of that, as the owner had said the same thing. She'd been planning to get settled in her house and take a quick trip out to the ranch, just to see it. Get a feel for the land and this new place she was about to call home.

But now there would be no settling in that house. What was she going to do with all her stuff? Her furniture, her bed, her boxes of Christmas décor?

The very idea that she'd brought the blue and gold balls was ludicrous. But Capri had lost a lot in Crescent Lake, and she'd held onto the stupidest of things simply because she could.

"Do you need a ride?" Gerald asked?

"No," Capri said, deciding on the spot. "Maybe you could help me unhitch the trailer? Then I can just leave it here while I figure out what to do."

"Sure thing," he said again, and he got to work. He had the trailer off and steady in about a third of the time Capri would've been able to do it, and gratitude swept through her. He would be in her gratitude journal that night.

She only wrote one thing for each day, but today would be the helpfulness of Gerald Neis. It had taken her four days to drive to Quinn Valley, Idaho from southern Texas, and each day she'd experienced a little miracle.

Gerald was hers today.

"Thanks so much," she said, forcing a smile to her lips. Such an action used to be easy, something she did without thinking. But now, after the indictment, the failed business, the lost job, the break-up....

Capri didn't have much left to smile about. And yet, God had provided a way for her to have at least one sentence of gratitude each day.

She made it back to the downtown area of Quinn Valley, enjoying the quaint atmosphere of the street. It looked like it had been plucked from the beginning of a Hallmark movie, and a sense of peace stole through Capri.

The hotel and spa sat on her left, but she went past them so she could check out the rest of the street, see what the town had to offer as far as shopping and dining. There was a pub, which looked promising, and a row of shops where she could surely kill a few hours on a Saturday afternoon.

If she wasn't too busy catching up on sleep or managing her brand-new business. "Yeah, you're not going to be shopping on the weekends," she muttered to herself. She'd probably be working. Getting new clients. Researching the fauna that thrived in this new place.

Her stomach growled, reminding Capri that she hadn't eaten since breakfast, and that had been on the southern border of Utah, eight hours ago. Up ahead, she saw a huge hamburger, with plenty of bacon hanging out the side.

Yep, that would be her first dining experience here in Quinn Valley. The Bacon Boys looked busy, but at least her truck didn't stand out among the dozen other pickups in the parking lot.

It was several years old, and the best she could afford. In fact, she hoped the prices for beef and bacon in this town wouldn't break her budget, as she was down to her last two hundred dollars.

"Be right back, Mols," she said to her black and white Boston terrier. "I'll get you something." But she probably wouldn't. She'd just feed the dog a couple of bites of her burger and most of the French fries.

It's okay, she told herself as she got out of the truck and headed inside. *You have a job. Starts tomorrow.*

And she did. She was meeting the ranch's owner at nine o'clock, and everything would be fine.

Her momma's words streamed through her head. *You're a real good girl, Capri. Everything will be fine.*

She'd clung to her momma's promises in the past, and she'd do the same thing this time too.

Inside the burger joint, the atmosphere was vibrant and smelled like everything Capri imagined heaven would. Cheese and beef and bacon.

And boys.

So many men filled the place that Capri wondered if she'd missed a sign somewhere. *Men only*, or *No cowboy hat, no service.*

Capri didn't fit either of those requirements, and she felt the full weight of every eye on her as she joined the line.

This place was obviously popular for four o'clock in the afternoon, and she anticipated having to wait several minutes to put in her order.

It's fine, she told herself, the eyes finally going back to their own business. Her head pounded, and her stomach pinched, but she studied the menu as if she'd never eaten a hamburger before.

She'd eat, and everything would be better.

Then she'd go to the hotel and figure out if she could even

afford to stay for a night. Quinn Valley Ranch had offered her a cabin as part of her pay, but she'd declined it. Maybe she'd need to ask the owner about that too.

Her head swam with all she needed to do and figure out. Capri wanted to bolt right then, but she held steady in the line. Her daddy had taught her that. Wait. Watch. Listen. Learn.

She'd be putting all of those things to use as she started her own landscaping company a thousand miles from the only home she'd ever known.

The door behind her chimed, indicating someone new had walked in. She turned to find a tall cowboy coming in alone. He exuded an air of importance, keeping her attention on him. A smile flashed across his face, making his strong jaw a little softer and lighting his eyes from within.

Oh, that wasn't fair.

Capri was well-versed in handsome cowboys, but this guy was in a league all his own.

She couldn't help how her eyes dropped to his left hand to check for a wedding band. He wasn't wearing one.

So he's fair game, she thought, immediately recoiling from it. She was not looking for a new boyfriend. She had barely escaped Texas with her most vital organ still intact.

She half-turned, expecting this handsome man to come stand right behind her. Maybe she could ask him what was good here, explain she was new in town, all of that.

But he didn't. Instead, he went right past her, almost to the front of the line.

"Uh, excuse me?" she said before she could even think.

In the Hallmark movie, the record would've scratched. The chatter in the place halted, and everyone turned toward her.

"The line's back here," she said, her eyes blazing at that cowboy. Just because he was good-looking didn't mean he could do whatever he wanted. Maybe it was the extreme hunger talking. Or the pounding headache. Or the fact that the house she'd rented—and put a thousand dollars down on —was filled with termites and completely unlivable.

Or, or, or. Capri could honestly come up with a dozen other reasons she wouldn't be putting up with a cowboy cutting in line.

"I'm sorry," he said, looking at the men he'd joined. "I was just taking a phone call. My guys here saved my spot." He had the charming ability to look confused and ashamed at the same time, that confidence still oozing off of him in waves.

Capri cocked her hip and then stepped around the few people between them. "Fine. My guys were just holding my spot too." She looked to his equally tall, hatted, and obviously baffled friends. "Right guys?"

"Right," one mumbled before turning back to the cashier and putting in his order. Capri stayed right with them, ordering when they all did. She cocked her eyebrow at the handsome man who'd pushed the wrong button with the wrong woman today—and watched in horror as he paid for everyone.

Including her.

So he really was there with those guys, and he was most likely their boss. "You don't—"

"You're one of the guys," he said easily. "Don't worry about it." Then he joined his crew at the soda fountain, never once looking back at her.

Capri huddled near the door, snatching her bag as soon as the teenager brought it to her and hurrying back to the safety of her truck and her dog. The burger tasted like manna from heaven, and with one problem solved, she went to take care of another, praying the hotel would allow pups for just one night.

THE FOLLOWING MORNING, SHE LEFT THE HOTEL MUCH earlier than she needed to. Her nerves fired on all cylinders, and no amount of positive self-talk and family mantras could soothe her. Aurora usually kept her up-to-date on such things, and while Capri had spoken with her sister at length once she'd made it to the hotel last night, all the good vibes were now gone.

The ranch was exactly twenty minutes north of town, and she eased her truck under the sign boasting that she'd arrived at Quinn Valley Ranch.

"Twenty minutes early," she muttered, moving slowly past the row of cabins on her left, paying close attention to the way she felt here. It wasn't Texas, that was for sure, but this land felt...tranquil. And that was exactly what Capri needed in her life right now.

A purpose. A place.

Next to her on the seat, Molly whined, her paws up on the window on the passenger side. Capri pushed the button to roll down the window, smiling at Molly's exuberance as she stuck her head outside.

She rumbled down the road and pulled up to the home-stead, a thin line of dust rising into the air behind her. She'd heard Idaho was cold, but this late in May, it seemed to be warm enough for her.

"Let's go," she said to Molly, and they got out of the truck together. No one had come to greet her, and she reminded herself that she was early. Before she could decide if she should go knock on the front door or just sit tight for a few minutes, another truck came down the road.

He parked beside her, and Capri's eyes met his through the windshield.

"Oh, no," she moaned under her breath as the tall, delicious, drink-of-water cowboy who'd paid for her dinner yesterday got out of his truck.

Her eyes flew to the porch as the screech of the screen door sounded. Maybe he was just here for something else, perhaps a visit.

"I got it, Dad," he said, his deep voice sending vibrations through Capri's whole body. He definitely wasn't just visiting, and he was definitely her new boss.

.

CHAPTER TWO

*R*hodes Quinn stared at the woman in his front
yard. Well, the front yard of the homestead,
which he would be taking over in the new year. Months from
now, sure. But the weight of it still burdened him.

The same pretty woman who'd first accused him of
butting in line and then let him pay for her meal. He almost
started laughing, especially when he caught sight of the
horror on her face once she swung it back toward him.

"You must be Capri Haywood," he said instead, working
hard to keep his face impassive. He took a few steps toward
the back of his truck to let Denver down. The golden
retriever was getting up there in years, and he could get in the
back of the truck, but getting down was a challenge.

His other two dogs—a German shepherd and a boxer—
both waited at the tailgate. "Wait," he told them, glancing
toward the front of the truck, where Capri still stood. She'd
said nothing, and he wasn't sure how much of a dog person
she was.

A little Boston terrier appeared at his side, and Rhodes
gazed down at him affectionately. "Hey, there."

"She's mine," Capri said, her voice coming closer. "Sorry. I figured I could bring a dog to a ranch."

Their eyes met when she appeared at the back of the truck, and a buzz started in Rhodes's bloodstream. Capri had long, blonde hair that fell in curled waves over her shoulders. Light green eyes that called to him to come a little closer. Get burned a little.

Rhodes felt like he'd swallowed straw. He hadn't been out on a proper date in a long time. Too long, judging by how he could only stare at the gorgeous creature in front of him.

"You can," he said, clearing his throat. "I have three, as you can see. How's she with other dogs?"

"Great," Capri said, holding out her fist to the Boston terrier. "Molly, sit down."

The dog sat right on down, and Rhodes couldn't help but be impressed. "So this is Denver," he said, using his dogs to hide behind, at least for another minute. Maybe then his pulse would settle and he'd figure out how to deal with his hormones, which were suddenly acting like teenagers and not the thirty-six-year-olds they were.

"He's old. Ten or eleven, and he can't quite get out of the truck by himself." Rhodes groaned under the weight of the seventy-pound dog and set him on his feet. "All right," he said to the other two. They both jumped down, Memphis barking once.

"The boxer is Memphis," he said. "The shepherd is Chicago."

"All cities," she noted. "I bet you get asked about that all the time."

"Yeah," he said, putting the tailgate back up. "I don't get off the ranch much, but I visited those cities once. Liked 'em." He knocked on the tailgate for some reason he didn't understand, a flash of embarrassment running through him.

He moved away from the back of the truck, from the

beautiful sight of Capri, from the rose-scented air around her. "So, you're here about the landscaping, right?" As if he didn't know.

"Right," she said. "And remember how I said I didn't need the room and board?"

Rhodes swung his attention back to her. "Yeah."

"Well, the house I rented is infested with termites, and I can't stay there."

Rhodes's heart pinched for her, but the idea of having her on the ranch really appealed to him. He schooled his emotions and said, "Well, you can have the cabin if you need it."

"I do need it," she said. "Is it furnished?"

"Not with much," he said. "I didn't go check on it, because I thought you didn't need it. But I can."

"I have all my things," she said. "I can take care of it."

Rhodes would look in on the cabin next door to his. One more thing to add to his list. He never accomplished everything on the list, and items were just shuffled to the top or bottom, depending on which fire he needed to put out first.

He stopped, watching the dogs run around the yard. "So my sister does a lot of the gardening here," he said. "But she's dating someone, and I wouldn't be shocked if they were engaged in the next little bit." He knew there would be changes in the family, and they were good changes. But it was still sad to see Betsy and Georgia move on. Find other places to be. He'd been at the ranch with his four sisters his whole life.

"My parents will be turning the ranch over to me at the end of the year," he said. "And I was told I have a grading problem with the yard here, extending all the way around the side and part of the back. When all the snow melted this spring, we had water all over in the basement."

"Oh," Capri said. "That is a problem."

"Yeah," Rhodes said. He didn't want to spend money on the yard, but he didn't see a way around it. He couldn't have water in the basement every time it rained. "So I figured I'd get the whole thing redone while we're doing that." He looked at Capri, once again struck by her beauty. "You can fix the grading, right?"

"Sure," she said, her voice maybe a little false. Maybe a little too bright. "I just need to learn my way around this town. Find out what equipment I can rent." She walked along the front sidewalk, and Rhodes went with her. "What are you thinking? Keep the trees?" She peered up into the huge trees in the front yard. "The pines are nice. I'm not sure what those are."

"Aspens," he said. "And yes, keep the trees." He nodded toward the flower beds along the house. "I hate those bushes. I want them all gone. Something else there."

"Bushes? Flowers?"

"I don't care," he said. "Something easy to maintain." He almost cleared his throat again but stopped himself. "I'm single, and I don't have time for yard work."

"So you'll live here alone?"

"Well, I still have two sisters who'll be here with me." Georgia wasn't engaged yet either, but he knew she and Logan had been looking at ranches. She'd get her diamond, and Logan would buy a ranch, and they'd build their own life out there.

Again, Rhodes tried not to feel too bad about it. He loved his sisters, but he knew they couldn't all stay at the ranch forever.

"You don't live here now?"

"No, ma'am," he said, ducking his head and pushing down on his hat. "I live in one of the cabins down by the entrance. You passed 'em on the way in."

"Oh," she said. "Yeah, there were four of them."

"My grandparents live in the first one," he said. "I'm next to them. You'll be in the one next to me."

"I'll—oof." Capri went stumbling forward, her foot catching on the step she hadn't seen.

Rhodes grabbed onto her arm to steady her, saying, "Whoa," like he would to an excited horse. Foolishness filled him. This woman was no horse. "You okay?"

"Fine," she said, a pinkness entering her cheeks that Rhodes really liked. "I didn't see that step." She glared at it, her eyes like lasers. "So let me get my stuff out, and I'll start taking measurements, making notes, all of that."

"All right," he said, having no idea what a landscape architect did. He didn't have to know. He'd hired Capri Haywood. "I'm not sure I ever said my name. Rhodes Quinn."

"Rhodes," she said, maybe a little too slow. Rhodes didn't know. His whole brain seemed to still be asleep.

"My sister will have coffee on in the house," he said. "You go on in anytime you want. I have stuff to do out on the ranch, but maybe we can meet later today and you can show me your plan."

"Yes," Capri said, tucking her hair behind her ear. A moment later, her dog came running over to her, and she bent down to give the pup a scratch. "I'll get it all put together for you, and we'll go over payment then too."

Rhodes nodded and whistled for his dogs to come on back to him. "Sounds good."

"Budget is...." She straightened and looked at him. "And I want to see where the basement leaked."

"Budget is whatever it needs to be to make the water stay out of the basement," he said. "And make the place look nice. I mean, I don't need a water fountain thing or anything."

A smile bloomed across Capri's face, and Rhodes sure liked the sight of that. She felt human and vulnerable, and Rhodes couldn't help the attraction flowing through him. Did she like what she saw too? Or would he always be the cowboy who'd tried to jump to the front of the line at The Bacon Boys?

"No water fountain thing. Noted." Capri ducked her head too, and Rhodes's heart did a little flip. She was *flirting* with him. No, he hadn't dated in a while, but he wasn't oblivious either. He wasn't stupid.

"I have your number," he said. "I'm going to give it to Betsy. She texts if she's making lunch for the day. Then you'll know." He surveyed the land around them, the sight of this ranch bringing peace to his heart. "I mean, you'll know because every cowboy and ranch hand at this place will start showing up right here, but yeah."

"Do you employ cowgirls?" she asked, and Rhodes looked into those clear, green eyes again.

"Several," he said. "You have my number too?"

"Yes."

"Great." He smiled and tipped his hat at her. "Text me when you need me to come back to look at...whatever." He started to walk away, almost desperate to get away from her so his mind would start working properly.

"Who can show me the basement?" she called after him.

He could, but he didn't want to. He had plenty to do out on the ranch, but he had time to spend here too. He turned around and walked backward. "Betsy can do that too. I'll text her." Then he turned and went around the side of the house to the four-wheeler in the back. "Let's go, boys," he said to the dogs, his fingers flying over his phone as he texted Betsy. "We've got cows to move today. Lots of work to do."

And lots of work meant he wouldn't have to fixate on the pretty blonde he'd just hired—and become next-door neighbors with.

❄

"Granny," Rhodes called later that day. His back hurt from where he'd been pressed into a rail by the throng of cows in the corral, and he rubbed the sore spot. His grandmother would have something to put on it. A salve, or a lotion, or an oil. She always did, and Rhodes had loved to tease her about her home remedies growing up. But now that he was getting older and his bones ached sometimes, he'd started to believe in her salves.

"In the back," his grandmother's voice called from the backyard. He went through their cabin and out the back door, expecting to see her out in her vegetable garden. It was almost too early to plant it, but she'd been out there every day since the weather had turned warm, getting the land ready.

But today, she sat on the patio, a glass of lemonade in her hand. "Rhodes," she said with a smile. "Come sit a spell."

Rhodes didn't normally sit until the end of the day. Even then, it was more like a collapse. He usually ate, crawled onto the couch, put something on TV, and fell asleep in the middle of it, all three dogs beside him.

He groaned as he sat in the chair across from Granny. "Where's Gramps?"

"Oh, he and Georgia went out to the family plots."

"Georgia loves that cemetery," Rhodes said. "Don't know what she'll do when she leaves this place."

"She'll just come back and visit," Granny said.

"Mm."

The silence carried them for a few moments, and Rhodes enjoyed it. He came to see his grandparents every day. Took them food if they needed it, arranged for errands to be done if necessary. Whatever they needed, Rhodes knew about it and did it. For the most part.

"Saw you hired someone for the landscaping," Granny said.

"Yep." Just the thought of Capri had his heartbeat firing on all cylinders again. Good thing Granny couldn't see through skin and bone.

"Maybe she's the one for you."

"Granny," he said with a sigh, though he'd been thinking the same thing. "Don't go all crazy."

"What?" she asked in mock surprise.

"You know what. You and your ladies are always setting people up. I don't need to be set up." He'd tried that, thank you very much.

"I'm just saying—"

"I know what you're saying," Rhodes said. "I'm behind. When my father was my age, he was married and had five kids. I don't even have a wife." He'd heard it all before, usually not spoken unkindly, but Rhodes definitely felt like he was failing the Quinn Family name. He carried a heavy burden about taking over the ranch. Having someone to pass it on to tripled that, and it was never far from his mind these days.

"Oh, here she is," Granny said, getting to her feet. Rhodes whipped his attention to his right, and sure enough, Capri came across the lawn, a tablet in one hand and a smile on her face. She embraced Granny as if they'd been lifelong friends, and the two of them came toward Rhodes.

He wished he didn't feel like they'd joined forces and ganged up on him, but that was exactly how he felt. Dread filled each breath, though he sure did like how Capri had swept her hair up into that high ponytail and that her jeans had smudges of dirt on them.

Unconsciously, he got to his feet, as if she were a lady he needed to greet from a standing position. Their eyes met, and a tether formed between them, telling Rhodes he was in very real trouble when it came to this woman.

And he needed a little trouble in his life.

CHAPTER THREE

*C*apri felt the world around her fall away, until it was just her and Rhodes and nothing else. She had the urge to push her hair off her face, but she didn't have any there. She'd pulled her hair back as the day had heated up.

She practically shoved the tablet toward him when she got close. "I have the mockups ready for you to look through."

"Oh, great," he said easily, like her presence didn't bother him in the slightest. It probably didn't. But the mere sight of him had all her cells singing, and she chose a seat next to him but pulled the chair back a few inches before she sat.

She swiped on the tablet while his grandmother said, "I'll go get more lemonade."

"I'm fine, Granny," Rhodes said, but she said, "Pish posh. Everyone loves lemonade in the summer."

"It's May," Rhodes whispered under his breath, and Capri smiled at him.

"She's great."

"I apologize in advance for whatever she might say or do,"

he said. "I mean, I love her, but she has a bit of a...streak in her."

"A streak of what?"

"I honestly don't know," Rhodes admitted with a smile. "But she'll ask a lot of questions and make insinuations." He sighed like he'd been through this before. "Anyway, just know that she's old, and sometimes has a frontal lobe issue."

Capri laughed then, the way it flowed from her throat so freeing. "Noted. Okay, so I did three approaches for you. Each fixes the problems with your grade, but each is a little different in its approach."

She tapped and swiped to pull up the first one. "This one I'm calling the Rancher's Paradise. It has benches for people to sit, and more flowers to make it feel more...luxurious."

Rhodes looked at the design while Capri's heart thumped in her chest. Would he like them? What if he hated everything she'd done? She needed this job. The cabin was small, but she'd decided she didn't care. Betsy had given her the key, and Capri could get her stuff inside that night.

With a little cowboy muscle, she thought, too excited to see Rhodes use his.

"I like it," he said, handing the tablet back. "Not sure how flowery I am, but it's nice."

"This second one is the Rancher's Roost." She put the tablet on the table in front of him. "It's more...functional. Grass and bushes you don't have to do anything with. The trees stay. No water feature, but nothing fancy about this one either."

"Okay."

"And the last one is the Rancher's Wild. It would leave you with grass for your yard, as normal. But the rest of the plants would be what you'd find naturally on the ranch. Native plants, bushes, flowers, and shrubs from Idaho. So it'll look more rustic. More like your house just sprung up out of the ranch."

He looked at that one the longest, finally lifting his eyes to hers. "Which one would you do?"

"Me personally?"

"Yes, you personally." He leaned back in his chair and folded his arms, making those biceps absolutely huge.

Capri swallowed. "I'd do the Rancher's Wild, but I love indigenous plants and making spaces feel like they belong in the wild."

"Great, let's do that one," he said. Capri's heart sang at the same time it sank. That model was her personal favorite, but it would require the most work. She didn't know all the wild and native plants of Idaho—yet.

"All right," she said, sweeping her tablet off the table and standing. "Tell your grandmother thank you for the lemonade, but I have to go get my trailer and get my stuff unloaded before it gets too dark."

Rhodes stood too, his dark blue eyes hooking into hers. How had she not noticed those eyes before? She felt like she was falling. His mouth moved, but no sound came out.

She blinked, and the world righted itself. "I'm sorry." Heat filled her from head to toe. "What did you say?"

"I asked if you wanted help."

"I can—"

"You're going to carry a bed and a couch inside by yourself?"

Capri wanted to, yes. She wanted to do as much for herself as she could. She didn't want to be tied to anyone, because then she went down when they did. Her first instinct was to refuse any sort of help. But her second was to accept it, so she said, "I could use some help."

"Text me when you get back. I'll come help." He started for the door of his grandparent's cabin, never looking back.

Capri stood in the backyard, wondering if he'd run away from her for the second time that day. Maybe he just didn't like to draw out conversations. Maybe he had to use the bathroom. Or maybe she'd just try to haul in what she could so she didn't have to embarrass herself any further in front of the handsome cowboy—who was her boss.

"Your *boss*," she muttered to herself as she headed across the back yard. "And your neighbor. And you don't want a new boyfriend, remember?"

Molly waited beside the truck, and Capri said, "Let's go girl," when she got there. An hour later, and after a mighty struggle with the trailer, she pulled back onto the ranch, a horrible screeching sound coming from the right side.

Panic hit her hard, and Capri checked her mirror to see she hadn't swung the truck out far enough and the trailer had hit the post holding the sign.

"No," she moaned, slamming on the brake. She didn't have money to fix the stupid Quinn Valley Ranch sign. She had called Parker Wescott about the house, and he had refunded her money for the rental and deposit. But still.

She sat in her truck, unsure of what to do next. Back up? Wouldn't that just grind the trailer along the post further? She should've found somewhere furnished in town to live, but Quinn Valley didn't seem to have apartments like that.

Someone knocked on her window, and she dang near jumped out of her skin. She spun toward the sound to find Rhodes standing there, and further humiliation squirreled through her.

"Want me to straighten 'er out?" he asked in that sexy cowboy drawl. She wanted him to straighten out a lot of things, her included.

"Yes," she said, putting the truck in park and hopping out. "I'm so sorry. The truck and trailer are new, and I don't really know how to turn...." She let her words hang there.

"You drove from Texas, didn't you?" he asked.

Pure exhaustion filled her, and Capri felt like crying. "Yes," she whispered.

"Well, then you did something right. Don't worry about it." He got behind the wheel, and Capri got out of the way. With the hand of a master, he got the trailer unstuck and around the corner without knocking anything down. He even backed into her driveway before hopping out of the cab like he'd done this type of thing dozens of times.

Which, of course, he probably had.

"What part of Texas?" he asked as he took the key from her and started to unlock the padlock on the trailer.

"Crescent Lake?" she asked. "It's just north of San Antonio. Little town out in the Hill Country."

"Okay." He opened the doors and looked inside the trailer. "I think this will all fit. I just went over to your cabin. It looked clean enough."

"Yes," Capri said, marveling at his steadiness. His calm demeanor. His kindness. "Betsy said she had it cleaned last week."

"And she showed you the basement?" He climbed into the trailer and started handing down smaller boxes.

"Yes." She lined the boxes up on the grass near the driveway. "She's great. I really like her." Betsy reminded Capri of her two older sisters, but she lectured way less.

"Betsy's awesome," Rhodes said, grunting as he moved the couch toward the end of the trailer. "You really don't have that much. We can get this unloaded in an hour, easy."

"You think so?"

"Yeah." He hopped down and added, "You go up and take that end of the couch. Then I can hold most of the weight."

She did what he said, and together they got the couch off the trailer and into the house. Once the bed was in, Capri just had her boxes, and they got those taken in lickety-split as well.

"Thank you," she said, knowing she wouldn't do much more that night. She'd find the sheets and fall into bed, because she'd never been so tired before. She knew the toll mostly came from her emotions, and her heart pined for Texas. For her sisters, her family.

"What about dinner?" he asked, and Capri's heart cartwheeled. Her long days and difficult decisions caught up to her, because her mind blanked.

"What about it?" she asked.

"Do you have food?" he asked gently. "I'm not great in the kitchen, but I can fry eggs and make coffee." He shrugged. "Breakfast for dinner."

Capri hesitated, the presence of this strong man in her small cabin almost too much for her. "I need to unpack," she said.

"All right," he said. "You do that, and I'll go start the coffee. Come over anytime." He stepped over to the fridge and opened it. There was no food inside. "If I don't see you in half an hour, I'll bring the eggs over here."

"You don't need to do that."

"The deal was room and board. There's no food here. I'll call for grocery delivery in the morning." He paused, seemingly at war with himself. "Yeah, that's what I'll do. I can't get to town tomorrow."

"It's fine," Capri insisted. "I totally sprung the whole staying-here thing on you. I can get my own groceries."

Rhodes stepped toward her, and Capri steeled herself to breathe in the musky, masculine scent of him. He'd smelled downright delicious that morning, and he did now too. "You'll get an allowance for groceries, Capri." He reached out and trailed his fingers down the side of her face. "I don't know what it took for you to get here, but I do know I can feed you tonight." A soft smile came across his face, making him even more gorgeous than he already was. Less tough. Less of a presence, though still utterly commanding.

He stepped back, letting his hand drop back to his side. "Thirty minutes. I'll make bacon too." With that, he left Capri to put together her new home.

She turned in a slow circle, the main cabin area not much bigger than the hotel room where she'd stayed last night. It did have two bedrooms down a short hall, with a bathroom between them, and was plenty of space for just Capri.

"Always just Capri," she sighed, wishing she'd labeled her boxes so she didn't have to dig through them to find her bedsheets.

CHAPTER FOUR

*R*hodes filled the air surrounding the cabins with the scent of bacon and browned bread, some of his favorite foods on the planet. He didn't start the eggs until thirty minutes had passed, because there was nothing worse than cold eggs, in his opinion.

Just as the eggs were ready to be flipped, someone knocked on his door. Granny and Gramps would've just come in, and there was no one else out here besides Capri. "Come in," he called over his shoulder, the layout of his cabin exactly the same as hers.

Kitchen along the back wall, island separating the area into a living room. His cabin was a mirror of hers, with his bedrooms to the left while hers went to the right.

She opened the front door and came in, wearing fresh clothes and a hint of gloss on those pink lips. Rhodes tore his eyes from them and focused on getting the eggs out of the pan before they cooked too much.

"Hey," he said, turning with the pan and putting it right on the granite countertop. "Everything is ready. I hope you're hungry."

"Yeah, I can see you made too much toast." Capri smiled, revealing straight, white teeth, and plucked a piece of toast from the stack.

"I have a weakness for bread and butter," he said with a grin.

"Is that your only weakness?"

"Hardly." He chuckled and swiped his hat off his head. "Do you mind if I pray?"

"By all means." She folded her arms and bowed her head, and Rhodes said a quick prayer, thanking the Lord for her safe arrival and the prosperity of the ranch. He generally prayed for his family too, but he wrapped it up quickly, not sure what Capri would think of him.

"Amen," she said after him, and her eyes immediately flew to his. "You have nice hair."

He ran his hand through it. "You think so?"

She stepped closer to him. "It's a nice color. Really dark red."

"All of my sisters have red hair too," he said, putting the hat back on. He wasn't sure if she was flirting with him or not. There was no smile, no giggle, no ducked head as she'd done last time. "So I made the eggs over-easy. I hope that's acceptable." He picked up a plate and handed it to her.

He scooped two eggs onto her plate and the other three onto his. He moved around the island to the bar, where he could easily access the rest of the food, and he sat on one of the two barstools. She sat beside him, and Rhodes felt a measure of happiness he hadn't in a long while.

Before he could think of anything to ask her, she asked, "You only have sisters? No brothers?"

"That's right. You?"

"No brothers," she said. "But only two sisters. They're both older than me."

"Still in Texas?"

"Yeah." She sighed, and it didn't sound happy. "My parents are getting older, and they're both married and live nearby. I did too, until—" She cut off so suddenly that Rhodes glanced over at her to make sure she was still there.

"You were married?" he asked.

"No," she said quickly, glancing at him. "Engaged for a while, but no. Never married." She did duck her head then. "You?"

"Nope. Never engaged either." He flashed her a smile, wondering what she'd think of him if he admitted he hadn't been on a real date with a woman he liked in over seven years. Did this count as a date? They were alone, sharing a meal together. Did that count?

He wasn't going to ask. "So you just lived nearby."

"Yes." She nodded and took a bite of her eggs before reaching for the salt and pepper shakers. "It was...difficult to leave Texas. I've been there my whole life."

"Why'd you leave?"

When she didn't answer right away, Rhodes abandoned his food to glance at her again. "I'm sorry. That was probably too forward."

"It was difficult," she said again. She drew in a big breath and blew it out. "These eggs are delicious. I'm rather helpless in the kitchen. Except sandwiches. I'm really good at putting together a killer sandwich."

Rhodes grinned at her. "Besides doughnuts, a good sandwich is one of my favorite things."

"Doughnuts, noted. How many bakeries does this town have?"

"Oh, just the one," he said. "But I don't get doughnuts there." He looked at her out of the corner of his eye to find her watching him too. "Granny makes the best doughnuts ever."

"So you'll only eat homemade doughnuts. You're a doughnut snob, is that it?"

He laughed, pleased when she did too. "Yeah, sure," he said. "A doughnut snob that cuts to the front of the line whenever he can."

Her smile disappeared, and she blinked. "I'm going to pay you back for that burger," she said.

"You really don't have to."

"I was...tired that day. Hungry. Broke."

"It was just yesterday," he said.

"Was it?" She blinked and wiped her hand across her face. "I'm really tired today too."

"You should take tomorrow off," he said.

"I can't," she said. "You hired me to do a job, and I'm going to do it."

"It's a couple of months, if the timeline I saw on your tablet earlier was right."

"True."

"So take tomorrow off." Rhodes honestly didn't care. He wanted to give this woman any relief she needed. "And the next day. Whatever. I haven't seen any rain in the forecast." He flashed a smile in her direction, glad that she continued to eat. He finished his plate of food and snagged a couple more pieces of toast before he got up and put his plate in the sink.

"Do you have horses to ride here?" she asked, and he turned back to her.

"Of course," he said.

"Could I...maybe do that tomorrow? I used to have a horse in Texas. I had to sell her to come here." Capri looked so broken, and Rhodes had the inexplicable desire to put her back together again.

"Sure," he said. "Want me to stop by and get you in the morning?" He wished he could suck the words back in the moment he said them. He sighed and ducked his head.

"That's probably not a good idea. I'm off pretty early. But I can come back and get you whenever."

"Can I text you?"

"Yep." He pulled open the fridge and gathered a couple of bottles of soda. "You want to sit on the steps for a spell?"

She took the soda from him, and he led her out the front door. They sat down side-by-side, and he twisted the lid on his soda, the resulting fizzy hiss so satisfying.

"Your granny is sweet," she said.

"Oh, she'll meddle right into your life," he said with a chuckle and a glance next door. "But I love 'er."

THE NEXT DAY, RHODES WAS OUT THE DOOR EARLY, AS promised. He liked to get some physical chores done when it was still relatively cool in the morning, and today, he met up with Flynn Hollister and Newton Matthews to get the horse barn cleaned out and all the animals watered until afternoon.

Then he had a meeting with his agriculture team, which Flynn headed up with Clay Martin and Joey Sorrel. After that, he needed to check in with Georgia about their pigs, and then his sister Jessie about the new calves and her plans for them. She handled all the calving and sales, and she'd had a very busy spring getting the calves weaned and out into pasture with their mothers.

Some of the work around the ranch was definitely seasonal, and Rhodes felt like he was drowning this spring. The winter was busy, but he went home before the sun most days—and that was saying something when the sun set by five p.m.

"Morning, boys," he said when he entered the horse barn to find Flynn and Newt already there. He pulled on his work gloves and picked up a pitchfork. "How was poker last night?"

"Jessie came," Newt said, an edge of glee in his voice. "And she cleaned Flynn out."

"She did not," Flynn said. "We play with Skittles, if you'll remember." He glared at Newt, but Rhodes just chuckled. He'd never felt like he wanted to come over and join in their monthly poker night, and Jessie didn't normally play.

"Who was she filling in for?"

"Betsy," Flynn said darkly. "Ever since she and Knox got serious, she's been ditching us."

"Really?" Rhodes went in the first stall, his men still loitering near the tools. "That doesn't sound like her. She loves poker night."

"Yeah, well," Flynn said, but that was all.

Newt finished with, "She loves Knox more, I guess." He shrugged, pulled on some gloves, and went in the stall next to Rhodes. He pulled the old straw out and put it in the wheelbarrow while Flynn finished his coffee.

"Who are you datin' these days?" Rhodes asked.

"No one," Flynn said.

"That's another reason he's surly," Newt called from his stall.

Flynn rolled his eyes. "I'm not surly."

"You look like you might bite my face off," Rhodes teased.

"Yeah, well, you would know," Flynn said. "The way you grump around this place."

"Yeah, but I own the place," Rhodes said. "And someone has to be the tough guy."

Flynn scoffed, but a smile twitched around his mouth. Anyone who got to know Rhodes knew he wasn't all that tough. He just didn't say a whole lot, so he came off as intimidating.

"I heard the landscaper arrived yesterday." Flynn finally reached for a pair of gloves.

Spontaneous heat leapt through Rhodes, licking his

insides. "Yep."

"So she's going to get the basement fixed?"

"Yep. We're going with an Idaho Wild theme."

Flynn paused, interest sparking in his eyes. "Really? What does that mean?"

"She's going to use native plants. Indigenous stuff." He really had no idea, but he figured he could repeat what Capri had said.

"Heard she's real pretty," Newt said. "She could be your next girlfriend." He pitched his old straw in the wheelbarrow too.

Rhodes's heart pinched as he looked at Flynn. He seriously looked like he was considering it. Part of Rhodes wanted to jump in front of him, arms outstretched, and confess that he had a crush on Capri already. The other part was taking the knowledge of his crush to the grave.

Way down deep. Forever.

So she was pretty. Had some bumps in her past Rhodes wanted to smooth out for her. Didn't mean she was interested in him. And compared to Flynn? Rhodes had never won, at least not with a woman.

"Nah," Flynn finally said. "I'm on a female fast."

Rhodes snorted at the same time Newt burst out laughing. He pitched new straw into the first and second stalls at the speed of lightning. "Right."

"No, really," Flynn said, moving past Rhodes to the third stall. "I need to clear my head."

"How long is this fast going to be?" Newt asked. "Maybe we should all do it with you, for moral support."

"I've been on a fast forever," Rhodes said. "If I meet someone, I'm not being tied to this."

"If you meet someone?" Newt swung his attention toward Rhodes, and when Flynn turned back too, Rhodes realized he'd said too much. "You never even leave the ranch."

"I do too," Rhodes said. "We went to lunch two days ago, if you'll remember."

"Boss, that was dinner," Flynn said, his full smile spreading his mouth. "And you *have* met someone. Who is it?"

"I didn't," Rhodes said, feeling his face heat. "Who would I have met?"

Newt looked thoughtful and then he snapped his fingers. "That blonde at the burger joint."

Rhodes scoffed, and it sounded pretty real to him. "I didn't even get her name. She scampered away as soon as she got her food."

"Yeah." Newt shrugged and went back to work. But Flynn stood there and watched Rhodes for a moment.

He walked toward him and past him to the fourth stall. "Stop staring," he muttered.

Flynn filled the doorway behind him. "Seriously, Boss. If you need...help, let me know."

"I don't need help," Rhodes said, more embarrassed now than ever. He wasn't fifteen, and Capri wouldn't be his first girlfriend. Maybe his first in a long time, but he wasn't so far removed from the opposite sex that he didn't know how to act.

"Thirty days," Flynn said loudly, backing out of the stall and going into the one he needed to clean. "No women for me for thirty days."

"Deal," Newt said. "And what should the consequences be should you slip up?"

Rhodes couldn't help smiling at the easy conversation between his friends, and he let that and the pace of the work sweep Capri right out of his thoughts.

She'd come to the ranch to do a job, not find a boyfriend, and Rhodes couldn't forget that.

CHAPTER FIVE

Capri slept for a long time, the cabin quite comfortable, though it was a new place. Her head felt fuzzy when he woke, and a tickle started down in her throat. She swung her legs over the side of the bed and groaned.

She could not afford to get sick. After getting up and getting in the shower, she felt a little better, the hot water clearing her sinuses. She downed a handful of pills and vitamins, hoping to stave off the cold with sheer determination and copious amounts of vitamin C.

By that time, it was almost noon, and she felt stupid texting Rhodes to see if they could go horseback riding during his lunch. He hadn't messaged her either, and Capri thought maybe she'd just explore the ranch a little bit.

He hadn't said she couldn't, and she was well-versed with the workings of farms and ranches. Texas had plenty of both, and her ex-fiancé had actually owned a boarding stable. She didn't want to think about Chase, nor the way he'd distanced himself from her the moment she'd told him about the legal trouble at the training facility where she'd worked.

The air in Idaho seemed to pluck thoughts of her ex-boyfriend and her ex-life right out of her mind, and she breathed in deeply. Down the lane a bit, the sound of singing met her ears, and Capri smiled at the simplicity of this ranch.

She opted to walk down the lane, figuring she could use the exercise. The road turned east with the homestead in view, and she turned to follow it. More outbuildings stood up there, and she recognized the familiar outdoor stalls for horses, the calving pens, chicken coops, and storage sheds.

The ranch seemed to be doing well, with structures neat and painted, roads flat and graveled, and people moving with purpose. Sure enough, she saw a couple of cowgirls going about their business, and she smiled.

She wasn't sure why she cared, but she liked that Rhodes employed more than men. "Can I help you?"

She turned at the feminine voice to look right into a pair of eyes almost identical to Rhodes's. One of his sisters, then.

"No, I'm just...wandering," she said.

The woman cocked her right eyebrow and leaned back, folding her arms.

"I'm looking for Rhodes," she said. "I'm Capri, the new landscaper, and he said I could ride a horse today."

"Oh." Recognition flashed across the woman's face. "You're Capri. I'm his sister, Jessie."

"Jessie, nice to meet you." Capri smiled at her, and they shook hands.

"He's around somewhere," Jessie said. "I know he was disgruntled about a lot of meetings today." She grinned like she'd just won the lottery. "He hates meetings."

"Who doesn't?" Capri asked.

Jessie laughed, and she said, "Right? Anyway, the meetings are out in the far barn. You could try out there. He typically hangs out near the corral after that." She nodded further east. "Both of those are that way."

"Thanks." Capri lifted her hand in a little wave and started toward a barn that seemed quite far away. No wonder it was called the far barn.

Her phone chimed before she'd made it halfway there. From Rhodes: *I'm not out in the far barn. Jessie was wrong.*

Before she could type out a question to ask him where he was, her phone rang, Rhodes's name springing onto the screen. Capri couldn't contain the smile as it touched her mouth. "Hey," she said.

"Why didn't you text me?" he asked by way of hello.

"Thought I'd get some exercise," she said, hoping she hadn't done something wrong. He didn't sound mad, but he'd definitely phrased his question as more of a demand.

"I'm down at the north end of the calving pens," he said. "I'll be done in a few minutes if you want to walk back this way. Or meet me at the stables."

"I'll walk toward you," she said.

"Great," he said. "Gotta go." The call ended in the next moment, and Capri looked at her phone in surprise. Rhodes was unlike any other cowboy she'd met before. Sure, most of them didn't say a whole lot. But she'd never dated the owner of a ranch before, and she couldn't even imagine all the moving parts he had to juggle.

So his brusqueness was normal. Expected.

She hummed a tune her momma used to sing to her as she walked back toward the barns and pens she'd already passed. Rhodes stood down at the end of the calving pens with Jessie, and both of them waved to her when they saw her.

Rhodes finished up a moment later and strode toward her, slowing the closer he got. "Hey," he said, that softness in his voice now. "I'm starving. Have you had lunch?"

"No."

"Let's go see what we can scare up at the homestead."

"I didn't get a text from Betsy."

"Me either, but there will be plenty of food there." He walked over to a four-wheeler and climbed on. "Have you ridden one of these before?"

"I'm from Texas," she said, hiking up her shorts and climbing onto the ATV behind him.

He chuckled and started the machine while Capri tried to figure out where to put her hands. His shoulders were too broad, and she felt awkward bear hugging him from the back. So she slipped her arms around his waist and held on that way, leaning her cheek against his back.

And wow, that ride back to the homestead was one of the best sixty seconds of her life. As Capri went with him up the back steps and into the homestead, she could admit that maybe she could handle another boyfriend.

Just because she'd come here for a job didn't mean she had to be exclusive to her work.

"Hey, Bets," Rhodes said as his sister turned from where she sat on the couch. "We're just here for lunch."

"There's some of that chicken cordon blue lasagna from the other day," she said, getting up. "And pizza from last night."

"You guys got pizza last night?"

"Oh, Jessie had a thing." Betsy looked from Capri to Rhodes. "Heya, Capri."

"Hi, Betsy."

"Is he making you work in this heat?"

"It's not even hot yet," Rhodes said, rolling his eyes. He looked at her. "Pizza or casserole?"

"Pizza," she said, which caused him to grin.

"Okay, I have to go," Betsy said, and she disappeared down the steps that led into the basement. Capri blinked, and she was gone.

"That was weird," she said.

"Was it?" Rhodes stuck a plate full of pizza in the

microwave and stepped over the kitchen sink. "What did you do this morning?"

"Nothing," Capri said. "Literally, nothing."

He grinned. "I'm glad. So we'll eat, and then we'll go saddle up."

"If you're busy, we don't need to go horseback riding," she said, a pinprick of guilt pushing into her heart.

Rhodes stepped toward her, closer and closer until he was in her personal space. "I want to."

"Okay," she said, looking up into those dark eyes, further deepened by the shadows from his cowboy hat.

"Okay." But he didn't move. Didn't back up. His fingers twined with hers, and sparks shot up her arm. The microwave beeped, and Rhodes jumped back from her as if his father had walked in and caught them kissing.

"Lunch is ready," he announced as if the beeping hadn't done it. Capri felt like she might float away, all because he'd held her hand for a moment.

But it was more than that, and she closed her eyes and said a quick prayer of gratitude that she could be on this ranch in Idaho—where she hadn't wanted to come.

She'd already put Rhodes in her gratitude journal for his kindness in offering her the cabin and helping her unpack. She had a feeling he'd probably get a lot of lines of her gratitude, and the idea didn't totally upset her.

AN HOUR LATER, CAPRI HAD TO ADMIT THAT SHE HADN'T been horseback riding in a while. Her hips ached, and every step sent a shockwave of pain up her spine. "I'm sorry," she said to Rhodes, when she'd asked to go back.

"It's fine," he said. Once they were back to the stables, he dismounted with the grace of a man half his size and reached for her. She practically fell off the horse, her muscles quivering from holding her in the saddle for so long.

"I'm really rusty," she said as he caught her around the waist. "I used to work at a boarding stable, if you can believe that."

"Right now, I'm disinclined to believe that." He chuckled, and Capri looked up at him.

"Disinclined?" She burst out laughing too, though her feet hadn't quite found their balance yet.

Rhodes joined in, and Capri couldn't believe how big of a twist her life had taken since her arrival in Quinn Valley.

Basically, nothing she'd thought would happen had happened.

She found her feet underneath her and looked around for Molly. "I better get home and get some painkillers." Her throat was itchy again, and she really didn't want to be sick. "I don't feel great either."

"Granny'll have some oils or something," Rhodes said, keeping her securely in his arms. He even swayed slightly with her. "Want me to stop by there after work and bring them over for you?"

"Sure," she said. "I can run to town too. I still don't have any groceries."

Rhodes brought her closer, his hands big and firm on her back. "Want to go to dinner with me tonight?" He dipped his head closer, making Capri's pulse riot in her veins. "We can go grocery shopping and get pain meds too."

"Sounds romantic," she whispered, not sure why she couldn't speak normally.

"Boss," someone called, and Rhodes backed up, letting his hands drop from her waist.

"Yeah?"

"Tractor malfunction out in field seven."

Rhodes sighed and lifted his hand. "I'll be right there. Can you get Clay over here?" He focused back on Capri. "Sorry, I have to get back to work."

"I'll brush down the horses and put them in the pasture."

"Thank you." Rhodes leaned down and pressed a kiss to her forehead. "Dinner, then? Like, six?"

"Yes," she said, "Dinner at six."

He grinned, tipped his hat at her, and strode away. Capri couldn't help holding onto the reins and watching that glorious male specimen walk away, his shoulders so broad and his boots so sexy.

She sighed and looked at the horse he'd ridden. A pretty brown mare named Ellie. "He's great, right?" she asked the horse. But of course, the mare didn't answer.

CHAPTER SIX

*R*hodes wasn't going to make a six o'clock dinner appointment. He knew it by four-thirty, and he texted Capri to ask if they could push things back. He didn't know how late, but Quinn Valley had an all-night grocery store, and they could get food and medicine even if it was ten o'clock at night.

She didn't answer right away, and that only put him in a worse mood. He swore, if one more thing on this ranch broke.... He sighed as he turned back to his father. "We need a mechanic if we can't replace equipment."

"Farm equipment is hundreds of thousands of dollars," his dad said from his perch on the couch in his office. His parents lived in the two-story house behind the homestead, and Rhodes knew it would be his house one day too.

"Then a mechanic," Rhodes said. "A trained one. In farm equipment. Clay is good, but he's ninety-five percent luck."

His dad chuckled, but Rhodes didn't see what was funny. "And I need him on the agriculture. Half our crops are going in late this year because of that freak snowstorm." He didn't want to complain. It never got him anywhere but angry, and his father didn't appreciate it. What he did appreciate, was a plan. "I'm going to put it on the job boards," Rhodes said. "I just need to find the time to get it done."

"Well, we've got one more cabin down in your row."

Rhodes nodded. "Someone should be able to drive out, too, if they don't want it. Maybe put them on full-time to check out everything we've got out here over the course of the first few months. Then, it could be just as-needed." He hated doing jobs as-needed, but the fact was, he couldn't put everyone on salary. He knew men needed steady work to support their families, and he tried to be as fair as possible.

A lot of ranches didn't have anyone permanently. They paid by the job or the week. So Rhodes would put this out there as a three-month full-time position. That would get them through the summer, when he really couldn't afford to have his machines breaking down.

"How's the landscaping coming?"

"She didn't work today," Rhodes said, thinking of the way he'd held her hand in the kitchen, and the quick kiss near the stables. His intentions were crystal clear in his mind, and he hoped in Capri's too.

As if summoned by the line of questioning, his phone beeped and it was Capri. *No problem. I just got up. I really don't feel good.*

"But she's going to be able to fix the lawn, right?" his dad asked.

"Yes," Rhodes said, typing as he talked. *I'm sorry. We don't have to go out.* But he really wanted to go out. He couldn't have her knowing his arsenal for dinner was bacon and eggs or canned soup. Not yet, anyway.

Maybe you could bring me something? I'm sorry Rhodes.

He imagined her saying the words, and something soft ran through him. *Sure.*

"Hey," his dad barked, and Rhodes jumped. "We're not done here. What is so important on that thing?"

"Nothing," Rhodes said, shoving the phone in his back pocket. "What were we talking about?"

"The yard."

"Oh, yeah," he said. "It's going to be great."

By the time Rhodes finished his meeting with his father, his chores for the day, and got Capri's shopping list, he was dead-dog tired. He'd been up for thirteen hours, all of them on his feet for the most part.

But he drove to Quinn Valley to get the things she needed, hoping he could maybe crash on her couch for at least a few minutes. Talk to her. Hold her hand again.

He wasn't well-versed in the grocery store, and it seemed to take forever to find the things on her list. He managed to do it, though, and he picked up several frozen meals for dinner. He'd decided he wasn't going to impress her with his culinary skills, so he might as well just reveal his flaws now.

Back at her place, he unloaded everything and put two meals in the oven for them. "Okay," he said, staring at the bottles of pills he'd bought. "What do you need? Stuffy nose? Sore throat?"

"Yes, and yes," she said miserably from the couch. He shook a few pills into his hand and took them to her with a bottle of water. She downed them, and she really didn't look great, what with those bags under her eyes and her hair hanging limply over her shoulders.

And yet, he found her beautiful in this vulnerable state. "You sure are pretty," he said.

"Stop it," she said. "I look like trash."

Rhodes smiled at her. "Pretty trash." He reached out and tucked a lock of her hair. "So I think I should get something out of the way."

"All right." She gazed at him, some inkling of anxiety in her expression.

He was the one who should feel anxious, but he didn't want her to find out from someone else on the ranch—namely one of his sisters. Sometimes they could talk and talk and they didn't even realize what they were saying.

"I haven't been out with anyone in seven years." His voice scratched, and he hated the words. Hated that they were true.

Capri started laughing, but Rhodes just shook his head.

"Oh, you're serious." She pulled in a breath, the nerves coming right back to her face.

"Yes," he said. "I'm serious."

"But...why? You're good-looking. Hard-working. Obviously successful." She waved her hand like the interior of this cabin screamed his wealth.

"I mean, I've been out with women, but I haven't had a—" He cleared his throat. "A relationship in that long."

"Fascinating."

"The ranch takes a lot of my time, and I'm afraid it's only going to get worse." He steepled his fingers together, trying to stay calm.

"Okay," she said slowly. "So I was engaged, but that ended pretty suddenly. I didn't think I'd want to date here in Idaho, but...." She shrugged. "You're kinda cute, and I kinda like you."

A smile burst onto Rhodes's face, and he chuckled. "All right, then." He started to get up, but she touched his hand and he stilled.

"Since we're doing some confessions tonight, uh, I have one."

"Shoot." Couldn't be worse than admitting he'd been cooped up on this ranch for close to a decade. But she remained silent, and Rhodes's anxieties went wild.

"I almost got sent to prison in Texas," she finally said, her eyes dropping to her lap. She picked at the fabric of her shorts, though there was nothing there to grab.

"What?" he asked, his imagination going wild. "Explain."

When she looked at him again, her green eyes practically shot fire at him. "I worked for a boarding stable, and the owner was moving money across the border. I didn't know about it, but I did help with the bookkeeping. The feds came in to shut us down, and we all got arrested." Capri swallowed, the topic obviously hard for her to talk about. "That's, um, the main reason I left Crescent Lake."

Rhodes didn't know what to say. He'd hired a money launderer. Holy brown cows. He stood up and sat down again. "Do you even know how to do landscape architecture?" He couldn't help it if his voice was low, scratchy, and slightly accusatory.

She'd just told him she'd almost gone to prison for smuggling money across the border. She could be anyone. From anywhere.

His heart tapped out a horrible, uneven rhythm in his chest. What had he done?

Too trusting, he told himself as they stared at one another. He should've asked for references at the very least.

Not only that, he'd started to feel things for her. They'd just talked about starting a relationship, for crying out loud.

Foolishness wove through him, striking like a snake when it hit his heart.

"I have a degree in landscape architecture, yes," she said, her voice quite icy. "I can get it for you, if you'd like to see it." She folded her arms, and part of Rhodes wanted to see the certificate and part of him didn't want to drive her further away.

"I believe you," he said.

"I haven't used it much," she said, quickly adding, "But it'll all come back to me, Rhodes. I swear. I will make sure your yard doesn't leak into your basement, and it will be the most beautiful, low-maintenance thing in your life once I'm done."

Rhodes swallowed, unsure of what to say. Capri obviously wanted and needed to be here. Could he be the one to make her leave?

He hated this part of being the boss. Making the tough decisions should fall to someone else. He didn't want to fire her, on a professional or personal level.

She twisted her fingers together into a knot and pulled them apart. "So? What do you think?"

Rhodes said a mental prayer real quick. *Please help me to know what to do here, Lord.*

Nothing came, which Rhodes took as a good sign. The Good Lord had always steered him away from danger, and feeling nothing was as good as feeling something.

"Let's give it a try," he said. "But if you get in over your head, you have to promise me you'll tell me. I won't be mad. I won't fire you. I just want to know."

"I promise," she said as the timer on the oven went off. "But Rhodes, I'm not going to get in over my head. I can do this job." Her eyes begged him to understand, to believe her.

And because he wanted to do both, he got up, swept a kiss across her forehead for the second time that day, and went to get their food.

A WEEK PASSED, AND THE YARD GOT TORN UP. TWO WEEKS passed, and dirt started getting moved all around. Rhodes tried not to even look at the yard when he went to the homestead, because it looked like a war zone.

He supposed everything did have to be ripped out in

order to be put back together again, and Capri had not said one word about being in over her head.

Rhodes felt like he was way in over his head, though. With her. He liked her too much already, and he'd been thinking about kissing her the next time they were alone together.

They'd spent almost every evening together since she'd come to the ranch, either sitting on his front porch or lounging on her couch. She missed a couple of nights after their confessions, due to a nasty sinus infection she sometimes still coughed from.

He'd told her all about his family—the dozens of Quinns all over the valley—as well as how things ran on the ranch. She knew most of his men by their names, even though she'd only met them a few times when they'd come to the homestead for lunch.

As the third week progressed, and some of the dirt seemed to be getting back where it was supposed to go, Rhodes realized he probably needed to warn Capri about the family Fourth of July picnic that took place on the ranch every year.

She'd be there, after all, and that meant exposure to all the Quinn cousins. So that night, he prepared to tell her a few more family stories as they ate ice cream bars on his front porch.

But she burst into his house while he was still toweling his hair dry from his shower.

"Guess what?" she asked, her smile positively radiant.

He grinned at her, thinking he'd like to sweep her into his arms and kiss her right now. "What?"

"Granny asked me to her ladies' luncheon for tomorrow." Capri actually bounced on the balls of her feet and clapped her hands.

Dread seeped through Rhodes at the speed of light. "Oh, boy," he said.

Some of her enthusiasm faded. "What? I'm waiting on the grader anyway. I can't do much at the homestead."

"It's not that," Rhodes said. "It's just...Granny has a way of putting her nose where it doesn't belong."

"Oh, she's a sweet old lady."

"As do all of her friends." He raised his eyebrows. "I can't believe you *want* to go."

"Are you kidding? It's a dream come true." She took a few steps toward him. "She reminds me so much of my momma." She stepped into his arms, her hands moving up his chest and eradicating his protests. "I miss my family."

Rhodes sighed, having no argument against that. "I know, but sweetheart, just be careful what you say, okay? There's a reason these ladies are the center of the rumor mill."

And he had no inclination to be the subject of anyone's conversation. Capri had been attending church with him and his sisters, so it wasn't scandalous. She usually sat beside Betsy and Knox anyway, and Rhodes kept close to his parents, Flynn, and Jessie. No one had caught on to their relationship around the ranch yet—except maybe Granny. She'd seen them sitting on the front steps several times, but Rhodes had never held Capri's hand out there. He saved those touches for behind closed doors.

"Come on," Capri said, and he realized she'd stepped out of his arms and retreated to the front door. "I bought mint chocolate chip ice cream for tonight. You said it's your favorite."

He had said that, and he did want to spend time with her. If only his stomach would stop churning long enough to enjoy the company—and the ice cream.

CHAPTER SEVEN

*C*apri licked around her ice cream cone, feeling like she was ten years old instead of the thirty-five-year-old she was. Her stomach buzzed with happy nerves at the nearness of Rhodes, this man who had come into her life unexpectedly.

They'd spent just over three weeks together in the evenings, and he still hadn't kissed her. She wasn't going to jump the gun and plant one on him, that was for sure.

"Capri?" he asked.

"Hmm?"

"Is your momma alive?"

She yanked her attention to him. "Yes, why?"

He shrugged. "Sometimes you talk about her as if she's dead."

Capri pressed her lips together, the taste of the minty, chocolatey ice cream actually making her sick now. "She's alive...she just doesn't talk to me at the present moment."

Rhodes had never touched her while they sat on his porch. Tonight, they were sitting on hers—and the back one, to boot—and he reached over and laced his fingers through hers. "Because of the fraud thing?"

"Yes," she whispered. "I talk to my sisters a lot, and they pass stuff on to Momma."

He nodded and went back to his ice cream, and Capri found it adorable and maddening at the same time. He was a quiet man, full of power, and confidence, and strength. Every once in a while, she'd like him to be full of words.

"Families are tough." He pushed the last of his ice cream cone in his mouth, and she got a bit of silence while he finished it. "Mine has a huge family picnic coming up in about a month. Three weeks. It's on the Fourth of July."

"Okay," she said. "You've mentioned your big family."

"Yeah," he said. "They're just different when they're actually all in person."

"I can handle crowds," she said, squeezing his hand.

"All right," he said. "Don't say I didn't warn you."

Before she could say anything, tease him about that dimple in his left cheek she liked so much, someone laid on a car horn on the other side of the house. Rhodes twisted as if he'd be able to see through the cabin to the road in front of it.

"I better go see," he said at the same time his phone went off. He stood and pulled it out and added, "Family meeting at the house."

"Go on then," she said.

"I'll text you later," he said, pulling open her back door and clomping through her cabin in those sexy cowboy boots. Capri smiled to herself in the fading light. There was still probably an hour until true sunset and dusk, but this was her favorite time of day.

Peace descended upon her, and she decided that she'd ask Rhodes if she could sit by him at church that weekend.

"Boy, then people will talk." She giggled to herself and

focused on the ladies' luncheon the following day. Jumping to her feet, she practically ran inside to check and make sure the dress she wanted to wear was clean.

It wasn't, as she'd worn it to church last week, and Betsy had made the most delicious chile verde tacos for lunch at the homestead. Drippy, saucy tacos, and the blue and white plaid had a spot near the collar.

Capri set it to wash and went back out to the porch to grab her phone. A blue light flashed, meaning she had a text.

Rhodes: *My sister Georgia got engaged!*

Capri smiled at her screen, her pulse accelerating a little bit with the memory of her own engagement. *That's great!*

She knew who Georgia was, of course, but she didn't spend as much time with her as she did Betsy. Betsy always had something cold to drink. She always had something delicious to eat. And the homestead had air conditioning.

Capri sat back on the steps, her sense of belonging in this state, at this ranch, with this family...strange to her. She thought she'd never fit in here, and she knew her momma was expecting her to come running back to Crescent Lake when she failed.

But she wasn't going to fail. No, she didn't have another job lined up yet. But she had a functional website, and this job had at least six more weeks until completion. She should probably get online or on the phone to make sure she could pick up the grader on Friday.

She didn't. She enjoyed the heat of the evening, and thinking about Rhodes, and she didn't want to admit that she hadn't ordered any shrubs or plants for the yard.

She should probably do that.

She sighed, deciding she'd try Momma one more time before she buried herself behind the laptop. While the line rang, she was secretly glad Rhodes had gotten called away tonight for a family meeting. She didn't have the heart to kick him out so she could research and learn what she needed to for this job, because she didn't want him to know she had to do the research in the first place.

She was not in over her head. She wasn't, and she'd said nothing to him. Instead, she researched after he left, and rented the equipment she needed, and slowly, she was getting this job done.

And it would be done right.

"Hey, junkin punkin," her dad said, and Capri brightened at the sound of his voice.

"Hey, Daddy."

"How's Idaho?"

She didn't answer, because a sudden lump of emotion had balled itself into the back of her throat.

"Baby?"

"Great, Daddy. It's great."

No, her mother hadn't answered her cell phone, but it was still great to hear her father's voice and listen to him talk about the weather they were having down in Texas.

THE NEXT MORNING, CAPRI DRESSED IN HER BLUE AND white plaid dress and stepped into black heels. She felt like a housewife straight out of the fifties, and she smiled at herself in the mirror. With curled hair and red lipstick in place, she went outside and down the front steps. The fourth cabin next to hers was empty, and she turned away from it in favor of the first cabin near the entrance.

A couple of cars were already parked in the driveway, and Capri's nerves vibrated a little bit. She smoothed down the front of her dress and squared her shoulders before facing the front door.

Up the steps she went, her heels clicking against the

wood. Before she could knock, Gertrude Quinn pulled open the door, a smile on her wrinkled face. "Hello, Capri, dear." She gave Capri a hug, and Capri closed her eyes and breathed in the powdery, minty smell of the older woman.

"You sure do look nice," Gertrude added as she stepped back. "Come meet the girls."

Three white-haired ladies stood in the kitchen, chatting and holding various drinks or snacks. Gertrude shuffled ahead of Capri, and said, "Ladies, our guest is here."

Everyone turned toward her, and Capri put a smile on her red lips. "Hello," she said, sounding too formal.

"I've seen her at church," one of the ladies said.

"She lives in the third cabin here," Gertrude said. "That's Maude, Nellie, and Ruby."

"She was supposed to rent the Parker house," Nellie said. "That's what I heard."

"Termites," Ruby said. "They've had an exterminator over there for two weeks."

Capri backed up a step as Ruby seemed to be yelling, and the words echoed around inside the cabin. Gertrude had hung pretty pink and yellow curtains on the windows, and her bar was topped with granite—and tons of food.

"Come on, girls," she said. "Get your bowls. It's time to eat."

"How are things coming with the Fourth of July picnic?" Maude asked Gertrude, who shook her head as if the world would come to an end that very minute.

"Oh, there's been some fighting over the food."

"Which Quinn is getting married next?" another lady asked, and Capri couldn't help smiling around at the ladies as they piled food into their bowls. It looked like a hodgepodge of items to Capri. Sliced pepperoni. Cheddar cheese cubes. Cold, steamed broccoli.

And when Gertrude started pouring what looked like

beaten eggs over everything, Capri caught on. They were making individual omelets. Sort of. She watched as the ladies put their items together and then poured their eggy mixture into a round pan sectioned down the middle. Gertrude slid everything into the oven once they were all ready, and everyone retreated to the dining room table.

Fresh flowers sat there, and the conversation moved as rapidly as the weather changed in Idaho—fast. She heard someone say something about what a family should have for a holiday celebration, to Charlie and Maggie's upcoming wedding at the restaurant, to how Rhodes really needed a girlfriend.

The conversation stalled at that point, and all four women looked at her. She picked up a sugar cube and dropped it in her coffee cup, stirring slowly while she tried to figure out what they wanted her to say.

Rhodes's warning not to feed the gossip mill ran through her mind.

"Oh, that boy," Gertrude finally said. "He's impossible."

"He's easily one of the most eligible bachelors in Quinn Valley," Ruby said. "I bet I have someone he can go out with."

"He won't let you set him up," Gertrude said. "I've tried."

"Pish posh," Nellie said. "You don't *try*, Gertie. You *do*."

"Rhodes is very stubborn," she said, reaching for the cream and pouring a healthy dollop in her coffee. Capri wanted to be just like these women when she got older, and she couldn't keep the smile off her face.

"You do." Gertrude scoffed. "Please, Nellie. You tried to set up your daughter, and look how that turned out."

"I made a bad judgement in character," Nellie said, her blue eyes firing at Gertrude.

Capri giggled, and that set off Maude beside her. Before she knew it, everyone at the table was laughing. The timer on the baked omelets went off, and Gertrude got up to get everyone's brunch out of the oven.

"What about you, dear?" Ruby asked. "Why don't you go out with Rhodes?"

"Oh, I don't know," Capri said, playing along and feeling more alive than she had in a long time. "He works really long hours, you know? Oh, and he's my *boss*."

"Pish posh," Nellie said. "That doesn't matter. I once dated my supervisor. Took him all the way to engagement." Her dark eyes sparkled like diamonds, and she leaned forward. "But that didn't work out. I had to quit."

Capri burst out laughing, this ladies' luncheon exactly what the doctor had ordered for Capri's soul.

"Well, I think you and Rhodes would be perfect together," Gertrude said. "And he hasn't been coming over here as often as he used to." She lifted her eyebrows, and she definitely knew that Rhodes had held her hand inside her cabin, though he'd been very careful not to touch her while they sat outside on his porch.

"I'm sorry," Capri said. "I've—needed a lot of help with the landscaping."

"Oh, *you're* the landscaper," Nellie said, as if she didn't already know.

"Nellie." Gertrude rolled her eyes and focused back on Capri. "Maybe feel him out, Capri. That boy needs a good woman at his side."

Capri nodded and promised she'd "feel him out." But what she really wanted to tell Gertrude was that Rhodes was no boy.

He was all man, and she couldn't wait to see him later that day and tell him about this conversation.

CHAPTER EIGHT

*R*hodes found Capri on his porch when he finally finished working for the day. Exhaustion pulled through his very bones, and he fell down onto the step beside Capri.

"Long day?" she asked.

He laid his head against her shoulder, a sigh his only answer.

"I made dinner if you want to eat."

"Yes, please," he said, getting up and following her over to her cabin. It smelled like roasted meat and buttery potatoes, and that was exactly what he got. They ate on the couch while she detailed how the luncheon went.

"And they want me to *feel you out*," she said, her eyes bright and joyful. "So." She took his plate and together with hers, walked it over to the sink. "This is me feeling you out. You wanna be my boyfriend?"

She laughed, but Rhodes actually did want that very much. So much. Probably too much.

He stood up and followed her into the kitchen, his smile

genuine on his face. She sobered as he closed the gap between them, his hands slipping around her waist.

"I'd actually really like that," he said, looking down at her and hoping he didn't smell too horsey. "So this is *me* feeling *you* out. What do you think of being my girlfriend?"

Capri swallowed, and Rhodes realized he'd probably come on a little too strongly. He just wanted to fall onto the couch, put on his police procedurals, and fall asleep.

But he'd also very much like to kiss Capri.

She still hadn't answered him, but he swept his cowboy hat off his head and dipped his mouth toward hers. She tipped her face up to receive his kiss, and Rhodes's heart felt like it was in a sprint it was beating so fast.

He kissed her slowly, trying to find the right rhythm. Thankfully, kissing seemed to be a lot like riding a bike, because he remembered how to do it.

He growled, drew in another breath, and kissed her again. This time, a little more forcefully. He brought her closer to him, enjoyed the way her hands came to his face and moved up into his hair, and fell a little further in love with her.

Rhodes finally got control of himself and pulled back, his breath a little labored.

"Wow," she whispered, swaying on her feet as her fingers curled around the collar of his T-shirt and held him right in her personal space.

"I'm thinking yes," he whispered. "I'd like to be your boyfriend."

She didn't need to tell him yes, because she kissed him again, and he got that message loud and clear.

SUNDAY MORNING, RHODES SLEPT PAST THE TIME HE normally rose. But he'd asked Flynn and Newt to take on the essential chores that morning, and they'd agreed. He tried to get out every morning just so he'd know what was happening around his ranch.

His father had, and Rhodes did not want to leave space in those boots. He was also finding it very difficult to do what his father had done, seemingly so easy. He wanted to know how the crops were doing, make sure the horses were getting trained properly, ensure the cattle got immunized on time.

Georgia had pigs and llamas to look after, and Jessie dealt with a ton of cattle-related things, and Cami took care of all of their accounting. Rhodes needed another vet on call, and he'd been dealing with a very pesky coyote problem that left him burning the candle at both ends.

Not to mention Capri....

He shot into a sitting position, grabbing for his phone. Capri had asked him to sit beside her at church that morning.

Church, which began in forty-five minutes.

With a yelp, he launched himself out of bed, his adrenaline pumping, and hopped in the shower. Twenty minutes later, he finished brushing his teeth just as Capri knocked on the front door and called his name.

"Coming," he called, grabbing his tie and threading it around his neck as he hurried down the hall. He pulled open the door to find her wearing a stunning flowered dress. Mostly black, the bright red, yellow, and green floral pattern was beautiful. She cocked her knee and lifted both arms above her head.

"It's new," she said, a smile on her face.

"Gorgeous," he said, pulling her to him for a quick kiss. "I overslept, and I haven't eaten."

"Grab something," she said. "I've seen you when you haven't eaten, and it's not pretty."

He grinned at her and walked back into the kitchen, grabbing a package of toaster pastries from the box and wishing he had time to make coffee.

His head pounded during the drive down to town, the little church where his family had been going for years. He saw a couple of cousins going inside as he parked. Capri didn't wait for him to help her down from his truck, but he did take her hand in his as they walked toward the building.

"This is going to start those rumors," Capri said.

"Yeah," Rhodes agreed. "Let's sit right in front of my granny." He grinned at her, feeling reckless and like he wanted all eyes on him—for once. But not really him. He wanted everyone to see the beautiful woman he'd somehow gotten to hold his hand.

Capri giggled and shook her head. "You're impossible."

"Stubborn, is what Granny would've said."

"She did say that," Capri said, stepping up onto the sidewalk and darting in front of him. "I need to tell you something."

He searched her face, finding a little bit of anxiety in those eyes. She wore makeup today, but not too much, and Rhodes liked the pink gloss on her lips. He wondered what it tasted like, and if he'd find out later that day.

"I'm in over my head at the homestead," she said, squeezing his hand. "I want you to come see the yard tomorrow and help me."

Help her? "I don't have any knowledge about landscaping," he said, his heart thumping in his chest. He did not want trusting her or hiring her to be a mistake. *His* mistake.

"I need your help," she said, and Rhodes couldn't say no to her.

"I can come this afternoon."

"Sure," she said. "Maybe we can talk about things before Betsy gets lunch on the table."

"Rhodes Quinn," a woman said, and he turned toward the

familiar voice. Jessie and Cami were walking toward him, and their eyes dropped to where Capri held his hand. They exchanged a glance with each other and joined Rhodes on the sidewalk.

"Are you two dating?" Cami asked.

"Yep," Rhodes said.

Jessie looked like she might cry. "Really?" She glanced at Capri, who nodded.

"What's wrong?" Rhodes asked, leaning closer to her sister.

Jessie looked back toward the parking lot, clearly at a loss. Rhodes knew this sister the best, knew what made her angry, and what made her smile. She was exceptionally good at games and auctions, and she had a bigger heart than anyone he knew.

"Excuse me a sec," he said to Capri, and he moved his hand from hers to Jessie's.

"You'll be late," Cami called after them.

"I don't care," Rhodes said, though the thought of sneaking in late with Capri got his pulse pounding. Such an action would really get the rumor mill churning. A safe distance away, he paused, his back to the others. "Jess, what's wrong?"

She sniffed and wiped her eyes. "Nothing." She usually wore her hair up, her face without makeup, and ranch clothes. She was natural in those things, but she seemed just at ease in her pretty dress and heels, her long, red hair flowing over her shoulders in soft waves.

"Jess," he said, almost a reprimand. "I'm not stupid."

"I just don't want to be the last one," she said abruptly. "Seeing all of you fall in love, and get engaged." She shook her head and sniffed again. "It's good. It's fine. I'm happy for you." She pushed against his shoulder. "Happy for *her*, because you're a great guy. I just...want a great guy too."

Rhodes squeezed his sister's hand. "Jess, you're not going to be last."

"Really? Because Cami got asked out this week."

"By who?"

"Malcolm."

"Oh, that's not happening," Rhodes said. "Malcolm's way too old for her."

"You hired him."

"Hiring him is different than him dating my little sister." Rhodes turned back to Cami and Capri, but they'd gone inside.

"He's not too old for her," Jessie said. "He actually *saw* her. No one *sees* me."

"That's not true."

"Let's just go," Jessie said, stepping around Rhodes and heading for the church. She muttered something about not needing dating advice from her older brother, but Rhodes didn't respond. He shouldn't be giving dating advice, and he knew it.

He waited for Jessie to slink past Capri and Cami before he sat on the end of the row with them. Capri looked at him with big eyes, and he shook his head. He could tell her about it later, if he told her at all.

He tried to listen to the sermon, but all he could think about was Malcolm dating Cami, and what was wrong with all the landscaping at the homestead. Each minute was painful, and Rhodes had never been happier to sing a closing hymn.

"OKAY," CAPRI SAID, HER TAN LEGS EXTENDING FROM HER shorts and into a pair of cute work boots. "So there's a problem here, with the foundation." She led him around the corner of the house while Rhodes tried to process what she'd said.

There, on the side of the house where he never came, was a hole against the cement foundation. Capri dropped down into it like she'd done it countless times before. "I can't in good conscience, just cover this back up and say it's good." She ran her fingers down a crack. "And I don't know how to fix it." She glanced up at him, worry in those pretty eyes. "We need a general contractor, or a foundation specialist to come look at it."

Foundation specialist. The words sounded like Japanese in Rhodes's mind. "All right," he said, looking at the crack in the cement. "I can call Coop Weston." His brother, Kenneth, had recently gotten together with a Quinn cousin, Katie. And Coop was the foreman for Pulaski Construction, who did a lot of work in Quinn Valley.

"Of course you know someone," she said. "Let me guess. A cousin?"

Rhodes mustered up a smile. "Brother of a cousin-in-law," he said.

Capri smirked at him, but Rhodes couldn't help it that he knew a lot of people in town, and that somehow, they always seemed to be related to him somehow.

"It could be normal shrinkage," she said. "But that usually happens around doors or windows."

She sounded so smart, and a twinge of guilt that Rhodes had immediately assumed she couldn't do this job ran through him.

Capri boosted herself out of the hole and dusted off her shorts. Too late, Rhodes realized he should've helped her. Their eyes met, and he let the helplessness he felt leak out.

"I know that isn't what you wanted to hear," she said, reaching up and cradling his face in her palm. "But it doesn't look too bad. It's fixable. We don't need to tear the house down or anything."

He nodded, glad for this moment where he could show his weaknesses and be okay with her seeing them. "Do we need to do anything to be ready for someone to come? I can call Coop right now. He'll send someone out tomorrow."

"I can meet them," she said, dropping her hand. "You don't need to be here."

Rhodes smiled at her. "I'm so tired," he whispered.

Compassion ran through her gaze, and a small, soft smile touched her mouth. He worked too much. Always gone from sun up to sun down, and then some. "Go home, then. Take a nap. I'll come get you when it's time to get up."

Take a nap. Rhodes didn't remember his father ever taking a nap. Ever, even on the Sabbath. "I think I will," he said. "You'll cover for me at lunch?"

"Totally," she said. "I'll tell everyone you're unfit for company because of the foundation."

He smiled, but even that took energy he wasn't sure he had to give. "Thanks, Capri." He'd driven to the homestead, so he drove back to his cabin, and Capri kissed him in the cab of his vehicle.

And then inside his dark, cool cabin, he slept.

CHAPTER NINE

*C*apri basked in the energy of the Quinn family, a perpetual smile on her face. Betsy put her to work in the kitchen shaving parmesan for the Caesar salad, and she did the job without problems.

Gertrude arrived with a slow cooker clutched in her hands, and Jessie and Cami rushed toward her to take it from her, their concern and love for their grandmother so good for Capri to see. Rhodes's parents entered through the back door, and Cami immediately went over to them and said something.

Jessie set the slow cooker on the counter and Capri asked, "What utensils do we need for that?"

"It's creamed corn," she said. "Slotted spoon."

Capri started opening drawers to find the bigger utensils, finally finding it next to the fridge behind her. She pulled out the tongs for the salad and a slotted spoon for the creamed corn. Betsy bustled over to the oven, pulled out the sliced ham, and slathered more sugary glaze on it.

"We're ready," she said as her mom put a couple of bags of rolls on the counter.

"Where's Rhodes?" she asked, and several people looked at Capri.

"Oh, he got some bad news and wasn't in the mood to be around other people."

"Grumpy," Jessie added.

"And tired," Betsy said. "I'll put together a container for him." And with that, their grandfather said grace, and the meal was served. A moment later, Betsy's boyfriend walked through the door with his twin, who was now Georgia's fiancé. She followed them and said, "Sorry, we're late."

"We just started," Betsy said, and Capri stood to the side with her, not wanting to be in the way of the real family members.

Betsy snuggled into Knox's side, and Capri thought they made a really nice couple. "What are you guys going to do?" she asked.

"Do?" Betsy asked.

Capri realized she'd opened her mouth and put her foot inside. "Oh, I—didn't—the homestead—" She clamped her mouth shut and glanced at Knox. "Um."

"Well, he hasn't asked me to marry him yet," Betsy said with a smile. "But when he does, we're going to live in his place in town." She looked up at Knox. "Right?"

"You've already got the yard redone, sweetheart," he said with a smile. "So, yeah."

"I didn't mean to imply—"

"It's fine," Betsy said with a smile. "What about you and Rhodes?"

Capri blinked. Yes, she'd spent some time with Betsy, usually just for fifteen or twenty minutes while she got a drink and cooled off. They'd talked recipes and the differences between Idaho and Texas. Not boyfriends—and especially not that her brother was Capri's boyfriend.

"Oh, me and Rhodes are...new," Capri said, hoping that summed it up.

"He's crazy about you," Betsy said, sucking in a breath afterward. Her eyes widened. "Don't tell him I said that. In fact, forget I said that." She grabbed onto Knox's elbow and said. "Let's get some food."

Capri watched them walk over to the bar and pick up plates, trying to get her brain to work properly.

"Whatever she said, just ignore it," Jessie said, coming up beside Capri. "Betsy sometimes doesn't know when to stop talking."

Capri chuckled, hoping to cover up her surprise. Of course, she knew Rhodes liked her. He kissed her like a serious boyfriend, and they'd only met a month ago. Capri tended to fall quickly, and she wondered if Rhodes did too.

He'd said he hadn't dated anyone in seven years, so maybe when he knew who he liked, he just knew. The thought terrified her as much as it excited her.

She really hadn't come to Quinn Valley to find a boyfriend —or a husband.

"Come eat," Jessie said, stepping forward. Capri went with her, the last one to pick up a plate and start loading it with food. She glanced around and took a seat next to Gertrude, who patted her hand with a smile.

"How was church?" she asked.

"Good," Capri said, though she hadn't heard too much of the sermon. The pastor had talked about finding joy among hardship, and Capri had lost herself to her own thoughts after that. She'd had plenty of hardship the last year or so, and had she found joy within those dreadful moments?

She wasn't sure. But she knew she hadn't quit. Hadn't moved back home and let her momma take care of her, solve her problems. She'd clawed her way back from the brink of disaster, and she now had a handsome cowboy boyfriend and a job.

Now, if she could just get more jobs here in town.

"What's on the agenda for tomorrow?" Jessie asked, and Capri glanced at her.

"Uh, we're waiting on some foundation work," she said. "So I don't know."

"I could use some help with the cattle."

A blip of anxiety moved through her. "What does that mean, exactly?"

"I go out and make sure they're in the right pastures. See if there are any sick cows. And tomorrow, we're tagging the new calves. Takes several hands." She looked at her with those dark green eyes, hope shining within them.

"Sure," Capri said, deciding on the spot.

"What are you going to do after you finish the yard here?" Jessie asked next, and Capri couldn't help but notice how Gertrude was listening in.

"I'm hoping to stay in town," Capri said. "I just need to find more jobs. Or maybe there's a hardware store or a nursery that would hire me to consult or something."

"Let me ask around," Jessie said with a smile.

A rush of gratitude filled Capri. "Thanks, Jessie."

"I'll see what I can dig up too," Gertrude said, and Capri grinned at her too.

"You guys are so great," she said, and she meant it. She did miss her family in Texas, and she decided she was going to try calling her mother again that afternoon after lunch ended. Momma couldn't ignore her forever, could she?

BY THE END OF THE WEEK, THE FOUNDATION HAD BEEN fixed, and the simple fix had made it into her gratitude journal. It had simply needed to be resealed, and the concrete specialist from Pulaski Construction couldn't find any other expansion or shrinkage in the foundation.

That had made Rhodes perk up, and he was back to his normal, confident self. Capri had gotten the land graded correctly, and now she just needed to get the earth back where it belonged, get the bushes and plants and flowers ordered and in, and order the concrete landscaping curb she wanted to make the property functional and beautiful.

She'd done a ton of research on native plants in Idaho, and she had a garden map drawn for the yard. Saturday morning found her in front of the laptop, ordering the plants and shrubbery she needed from a bigger nursery in Lewiston. She could borrow a truck from the ranch to go pick everything up, and for the first time since she'd arrived in Idaho, Capri felt like things were coming together.

Her phone rang, and she didn't recognize the number. Her first instinct was to ignore the call, because she didn't like talking to strangers. Then she realized she'd asked Jessie and Gertrude to help her drum up business. And this call could be her next client.

"Hello?" she asked, focusing on the call instead of the nursery's inventory.

"Is this Capri Haywood?"

"Yes, sir," she said, putting in some Texas twang. "How can I help you?"

"I have a house I'm looking to rent out, but the yard needs some serious work. Gertie Quinn said you could help me with that."

"I can," Capri said, clicking quickly to open a new email so she could get his name and number. "Let's get some info from you, and I'll come take a look next week." She got his name, number, and address, and set up a time to get to the property and make her initial assessment.

She hung up and immediately searched for how to give a quote for yard work. She needed forms, and a clipboard, and probably a way to distinguish herself as the professional.

"A t-shirt," she muttered, wondering if she could get a custom company tee made before next week. After falling down the rabbit hole with company logos and the merchandise she could buy for a good hour, she pulled herself back to reality.

"Plants," she muttered, getting back to the tab for the nursery in Lewiston. She still didn't have everything lined up and ordered before Rhodes messaged and asked her to come to the horse barn and go riding with him.

She didn't think twice. She changed out of her pajamas and pulled on a pair of cowgirl boots before spraying herself with sunscreen and heading out the door, Molly right at her heels. She drove over to the horse barn, because the heat was no joke. It wasn't Texas heat, but it still burned right through her fair skin.

Her shoulders had freckled since working outside, and Rhodes had teased her about it a couple of times. He greeted her with a grin as he came out of the barn.

"Hey, pretty lady." He swept his arm around her and pulled her right against his chest, his cowboy hat bumping against her forehead as he kissed her. Capri let herself get swept away in the scent of this man, the slow, sensual way he kissed her. She pressed into him, deepening the kiss and forgetting completely that they weren't in the privacy of her cabin. Or his. Or his truck. Or the side of the house.

Rhodes seemed to like to kiss her wherever he could, and Capri certainly wasn't complaining.

"Hey," a man called. "Take it inside."

Rhodes ducked his head, a smile on his face as he turned toward Flynn, one of his best friends and most trusted cowboys.

"How many more days?" he called to Flynn, who laughed.

"None," he said. "Yesterday was day thirty." He waved as he disappeared into the barn.

"What's he talking about?" Capri asked.

"Oh, he went on a female fast," Rhodes said. "I don't believe for a second he lasted all thirty days. But whatever."

Capri giggled, linked her hand with Rhodes's, and asked, "So where are we riding today?"

"I need to get out to a well and check it."

"Ooh, wells are my favorite."

Rhodes chuckled, just like Capri knew he would. "You say everything is your favorite," he said.

"Well, is it so bad to have a lot of favorites?"

"Actually, yes," he said, leading her into the barn and through to the stables. "For example, if your boyfriend wanted to buy you a gallon of your favorite ice cream, he wouldn't know what to get if you have a half-dozen favorites."

"A half-dozen?" she asked. "You're exaggerating."

"Am I? You said mint chocolate chip was your favorite. Then the caramel pecan. Then that double chocolate moose tracks."

"Hey, that was delicious. It had brownies *and* fudge-filled hoof prints."

Rhodes laughed, and Capri felt herself slipping down a slippery slope toward falling in love with him. "And last night, if you'll recall, your favorite ice cream was...." He paused, his eyebrows raised.

"Orange sherbet," they said together. He gave her a look that said, *There you go. I'm right.*

And maybe he was right.

"Well," she said as he got down the saddles. "Maybe my boyfriend should surprise me. Has he thought of that?"

"He has," Rhodes said, grinning at her. "And then he

bought something he felt sure was your favorite." He turned toward her, a tall tube of bath bombs in his hand.

Capri's eyes widened as her smile stretched across her face. "Rhodes," she said, taking the gift. "Thank you." She threw her arms around him and kissed him, a little sloppily at first, then aligning their lips perfectly.

"What's the occasion?" she asked.

"We've been together a month," he said. "And well, since that's a long time for me, I wanted to celebrate."

Capri found him to be the sweetest, kindest man she'd ever met. So she kissed him again and said, "Let's get out to that well, so I can get back and relax with these bath bombs."

Rhodes chuckled and stepped back, his head still ducked. "Capri...I...I sure do like you. It's been a great month for me."

Their eyes met, and Capri basked in the desire in his eyes, the complete confidence in how he felt streaming from his eyes.

She grinned at him, joy exploding through her. "I sure like you too, Rhodes."

But in her mind, she was halfway to love—and she needed to pull back on the reins before she lost her heart again.

CHAPTER TEN

*R*hodes loved walking to work in the pre-dawn hour before the sun rose. There was something tranquil and beautiful about his land at that time, and he breathed in the air of what was sure to be a hot day.

He'd made it through the Quinn Family Fourth of July picnic a few days ago. The ranch was back to normal, with the big tent taken down and all the tables folded and put away. He loved his family, though they were loud and obnoxious sometimes.

And Betsy had gotten engaged.

Rhodes felt two steps closer to moving from the cabin where he'd lived for eighteen years, and he wasn't sure how he felt about it. He didn't need the homestead, with its four thousand square feet, two kitchens, and impossible to keep clean shelves.

He barely cleaned his own cabin. It had two bedrooms, and that was plenty for him right now. Even if he got married tomorrow, he wouldn't need more than two bedrooms for years. And he certainly wasn't going to get married tomorrow.

Yes, he and Capri were serious. He hadn't met anyone he liked even a tenth of much in the past several years. She kissed him like she liked him too—had even said it out loud a week or two ago.

But with two of his four sisters engaged now—and leaving the homestead and the ranch—he felt like he was one step closer to taking over the huge house. Cami and Jessie both lived downstairs as it was. He could move in upstairs and still have three times as much space as he had in his cabin.

Space wasn't an issue for Rhodes. It was the responsibility that came along with moving into the homestead. He'd miss Granny and Gramps being so close, and he'd have to admit that there wasn't anyone but him to answer to when it came to the house, the land, the ranch, the animals, all of it.

That knowledge pressed down upon him like a ton of bricks, and he wasn't entirely comfortable with it.

He walked along the chicken coops, finding the work there done. Newt was great at fulfilling his assignments, and Rhodes could ask him to do anything, and he'd do it. Just the kind of cowboy Rhodes needed at Quinn Valley Ranch.

And he had several, as he found the calves had all been watered as well, and Jessie was currently holding a bottle to the mouth of one particular runt she had a soft spot for. Rhodes approached, noticing her hat sat a little sideways on her head.

"Hey," he said, glancing around. "You seen Flynn?"

"Why would I have seen Flynn?" she demanded, her eyes widening. A flush worked its way up her neck, and Rhodes frowned.

"Um, he works right over there in the morning. Don't you always see Flynn in the morning?" He nodded toward the corral where they kept a few cows who couldn't seem to get along with the herd out on the range.

"Right." Jessie ducked her head. "I think he went over to the hay barn with Clay. Something about shoes. They were going to call Knox."

"Thanks," Rhodes said, already tired and the day's problems hadn't even begun yet. If there was something wrong with the horseshoes and they needed to call Knox, Rhodes almost didn't want to know about it.

But find out about it, he did. Flynn told him about the pesky horse that wouldn't stop bucking his shoes against the wall, and Rhodes considered the tall, black horse they'd acquired last year.

Rhodes loved horses, everything about them. He reached his palm toward Inkblaster, and said, "What are you doin', huh? They're just shoes. You've been wearing 'em your whole life."

The horse pushed his nose against Rhodes's palm, and he said, "I'm taking him out."

"You're going to make him think he can kick a hole in his stall and then go for a ride," Flynn said.

Before Rhodes could answer, or even turn to go get a saddle, the door to the stables burst open. "Boss, there are six wolves already across the north fence." Monson Jackson stood there, his chest heaving as if he'd run all the way from the fence line himself. Of course he hadn't, but Rhodes felt the same adrenaline spiking in his system.

"Saddle up," he said without missing a beat. "Clay, you and Flynn come with me on the ATV." They took off for the homestead, where the family owned a few ATVs. Several minutes later, he met up with his scouting team that had been out in the remote cabin last night.

"Status," he barked, scanning the horizon for any signs of wildlife. He couldn't even see their cows.

"Seven down, Boss," Gil said. "We pushed the wolves back and set up temporary fencing. They seem hungry though."

Rhodes refused to let the sigh building in his chest come out. "Okay," he said. "Let's wait for our backup team, and then we'll get them out and reinforce the fences. Clay, let's start moving the cattle west."

"On it," Clay said.

"It'll take three days to move the herd," Flynn said, stepping next to him, also looking out onto the ranch."

"Yep," Rhodes said. "But I'm not losing seven a night by leaving them here." He glanced at his best friend. "What else should we do?"

"Call Wildlife Management," he said.

"I'm assuming Monson did that," Rhodes said. He hadn't even thought to ask.

"He did, Boss," Gil said, bending to pluck a piece of long grass and sucking on it. "Just heard on the radio that they're on their way."

"So we hold tight," Rhodes said. "Get our supplies out here. Move the heard. See what Wildlife Management says."

The men with him nodded. Gil wandered over to his horse and started checking something in his saddlebag, and Rhodes pushed his cowboy hat further over his ears, already hot and it was barely eight a.m. Exhaustion swept through him, but it was going to be a long day, and he didn't have time for naps. Or texts. Or daydreams about his girlfriend.

All thoughts of those fled when Flynn said, "I may have broken my female fast a few days early."

Rhodes swung his attention to him, a smile spreading his whole face. "I knew it."

Flynn looked at him, but Rhodes didn't see the happy-go-lucky man he usually did, with sparkling eyes and a secret about who he was dating this time. "It's your sister."

Confusion puckered Rhodes's eyebrows. "What?"

"I started seeing your sister," he said.

"Cami has a boyfriend," Rhodes said.

"It's not Cami." Flynn walked away, and Rhodes stared after him, sure he'd heard wrong.

Jessie? She wouldn't touch Flynn with a ten-foot pole. Would she?

He spun in a slow circle, so many things lining up now. She'd acted so weird earlier when he'd asked about Flynn. And he couldn't say he was upset about Jessie and Flynn... other than Flynn seemed to flit from woman to woman the way Capri changed her favorite flavor of ice cream.

Since he was sitting tight anyway, he pulled out his phone and called his sister. "Heya, Jess," he said, turning his back on Flynn. He had no idea what to say next. He didn't talk much about his love life with his sister, and neither did she.

"I heard a rumor that you have a boyfriend," he said.

"I'm going to kill Flynn," she said, her voice full of bite. "He promised me he wouldn't tell you."

"It's a secret?"

"No, I just...." She exhaled heavily. "It's *Flynn*."

"He's a good man," Rhodes said. "I'm not upset about it." Not that he thought his strong-willed sister would care what he thought about her boyfriend, whether it was Flynn or not.

"I gotta go," Jessie said, and the line went dead. Rhodes sighed, feeling like he'd messed up somehow. Again. He couldn't seem to get anything right these days.

Wildlife Management arrived a few minutes later, and he had to focus from then on. He listened. Asked questions. Set men to work when he needed to, and generally gave everything he had to this ranch.

Just like he always did.

When he got home, the sun had set already. He still saw the piece of paper taped to his door, flapping in the slight breeze.

Come let me know you're alive. -Capri

He frowned and glanced next door. Light shone out her windows, and while Rhodes didn't want to do anything but eat and fall asleep, he went next door and knocked.

She pulled open the door, looking fresh and clean, probably right out of the tub if the scent of lavender and oranges coming off her skin was any indication. "There you are. I called you at least five times."

"I'm sorry," he said. "I was real busy today."

"Mm hm." She didn't look happy, but Rhodes didn't know what to do about it. This was his life. It wasn't going to get easier or less time-consuming. "Granny wanted you to go to town, but I did it for you."

"What for?"

"It's Friday," she said, as if that should mean something. And all at once, it did.

"Her hair appointment," he said, his shoulders slumping. "I was supposed to pick her up."

"That's right," she said. "And no one could find you on the ranch, and you should text me if you're going to go so far out you don't have service."

"I was dealing with wolves on the north fence."

"That doesn't make me feel any better." Capri turned and walked into her cabin, leaving the front door open. Rhodes sighed, went inside, and closed the door behind him.

"I'm sorry," he said. "I should've texted you."

"You work too much," she said over her shoulder.

"It's my ranch."

"Right, but Rhodes, you don't have to leave before the sun rises to make sure the chickens are fed." She faced him, her arms folded and those green eyes that he'd fallen in love with blazing fire at him. "Has Newt ever *not* fed and watered the chickens?"

"No," he said slowly.

"Right," she said again. "So you don't actually have to leave your cabin until eight or nine in the morning. Why do you leave by five?"

CHAPTER ELEVEN

Rhodes had no answer for her, and that only added fuel to the angry fire in her heart. She drew in a deep breath and blew it out, forcing some of the frustration to go with it.

"You're going to burn yourself out," she said in a much calmer, gentler voice. She uncrossed her arms, wishing everything inside her didn't feel laced so tight, and stepped over to the fridge. "I have dinner for you."

"I can make my own dinner," he said darkly, and Capri glanced at him.

"Fine." She walked across the room and handed him the plastic container. "Take it. Go heat it up."

He did take it, but he didn't leave. "I don't want you to be upset with me."

Capri didn't want to give him an ultimatum. In her experience, those were never good. Never turned out well. She searched that handsome face she'd been worried about for hours, and reached up to touch his jaw.

"You work too much," she said again. She didn't want it to be a thing between them, but it definitely was. Things with Rhodes were serious, and Capri knew it. He was kind and thoughtful, sure. He'd made her feel like a queen on their one-month anniversary, doing and saying everything right.

That came from his heart, not him trying to impress her. She knew that.

But she also knew he could not last for years working as much as he did. And she didn't want a husband who left at five o'clock in the morning and didn't come home until after dark. She wanted to wake up next to him, not wake up and find him gone.

She wanted to eat her way through every ice cream flavor on the planet with him beside her on the steps while they talked. She couldn't do that if he was still out on the ranch. Of course he needed to work. But he didn't need to work sixteen hours a day.

"I'm sorry," he said again. "I'll try to find a balance."

Capri nodded, because she didn't know what else to do. He'd apologized. "You want me to heat that up for you?"

He handed it back. "Yes, please." He turned toward the couch and sank onto it while she moved into the kitchen and stuck the plastic container in the microwave. The thudding of his boots being kicked off met her ears, and she filled a glass with ice and then water for him.

Her plants had come in at the nursery in Lewiston that day, and she needed a truck tomorrow to go pick them up. "Hey, so, I have a favor."

Rhodes didn't answer, and Capri turned toward him, her fingers still clutching the cold glass. She walked over to the couch to find Rhodes fast asleep. Something softened in her though she wanted to throw the ice water in his face to wake him up. Talk to her. Help her.

To be safe, she turned and put the glass on the dining room table before going around the couch and sitting in the recliner opposite Rhodes. He was so beautiful, all the cares and worries gone from his face.

Capri sighed as the microwave beeped, indicating his dinner was ready. She didn't move. Instead, she whispered, "Things are going so great at the homestead. I can do this job. Not only that, I got that contract signed out at the Huntsman's place. Yard work every week in the summer. Every other in the spring and fall."

She pretended like he'd smiled back at her, told her that was great.

"Yeah," she continued the one-sided conversation with herself. "It might not pay for a house in town, but I can find other jobs. I'm going to ask at the nursery tomorrow."

Good idea, he'd say.

"And by the way, is there a truck I can borrow to go pick up your plants? Mine's full of tools, and it'll be hard to clean it out and get to the nursery on time."

Of course, he'd tell her. Then he'd take her into his arms and kiss her, whisper how much she meant to him, and thank her for dinner.

Capri closed her eyes, her fantasies much better than her reality of her snoozing cowboy boyfriend on the couch.

CAPRI WOKE TO THE SOUND OF A DOOR CLOSING. SHE SAT up and called, "Rhodes?" but he didn't answer.

Moving quickly, she got out of bed and hurried to the window. Sure enough, she caught sight of a silhouette moving from her house toward his. She hadn't had the heart to wake him last night, so she'd left him sleeping on her couch when she'd gone to bed.

She returned to bed, sinking down onto the mattress with a sigh. Maybe she shouldn't have been so forward with

Rhodes. She was a new part of his life, and it was clear the man had a routine for his work. Who was she to disrupt it? Tell him he should do something different?

Her phone brightened, showing her that it was just after two in the morning. The message that popped up was from Rhodes.

I'm so sorry I fell asleep on your couch. Thank you for taking care of me. <3

That soft feeling moved through her again, and Capri sent the heart emoji right back to him.

I woke you, didn't I?

No, it's fine, she tapped out.

I don't have to walk by the chickens to make sure they're fed every morning.

I know you don't.

The fact was, he *liked* doing it. Rhodes enjoyed being everywhere on the ranch, knowing everything. He thought it was his job.

"He could benefit from some delegation lessons," she muttered. But it wasn't like she had everything figured out. Her mother still wouldn't talk to her, despite Capri's attempts at texts and phone calls.

She'd told her about the job here, and how well it was going. She'd told her about the new contract she'd put in place yesterday. Maybe she'd never be good enough for her mother again.

And she didn't want Rhodes to feel like that about her.

"Dinner tonight?" she whispered as she typed out the message.

Yes, he said. *Before dark, I promise.*

Before dark, she sent back to him, finally lying down and closing her eyes, her phone pressed right over her heart.

Rhodes did show up for dinner at her place before dark, as promised. He even smelled like woodsy cologne, with that damp hair peeking out from underneath his sexy cowboy hat.

"You didn't cook," he said, glancing inside while she crowded him back onto the front porch.

"Nope." She stretched up to kiss him, intending it to be quick, because she was starving, and it was Saturday night. Everywhere in town would be busy, and while he had arrived before dark, it was definitely dinnertime.

But Rhodes encircled her in his arms and slowed her right down, taking his time as he kissed her. And kissed her. And kissed her. "Mm, I missed you," he said, moving his mouth to her neck.

Capri held onto those shoulders and enjoyed the fluttery sensations moving through her bloodstream. Finally, she said, "Come on, cowboy. Anyone could see us."

"I don't care," he whispered, touching his mouth to hers again. "But I am hungry."

"Me too." She pushed gently on his chest, and he backed up a couple of inches. "I want to go to the pub. I hear the food is great, and we have to get off this ranch."

He cocked his head. "We do?"

"Rhodes," she said. "It is not healthy to go from here to the homestead and back. Nowhere else."

"You went to pick up Granny at her hair appointment yesterday."

"And that made me realize how good it is to get out of here sometimes." She smiled at him and led him down the steps. "Do you want to drive?"

"Yeah, I'll drive." He didn't sound enthused about going to town, or the pub, but Capri had a seething need for a change of scenery.

The pub was busy, and they had to wait for a table. Capri didn't mind. She rather liked the loud music and the vibrant atmosphere. "Have you eaten here before?" she asked.

"Ryder and Maggie own this place," he said. "Remember how we had all those baked beans last weekend for the Fourth?" He pointed to the menu. "Right there."

"Of course," Capri said. She should've known. She'd met a lot of the Quinns last weekend, but she hadn't memorized all their names, nor what they did for a living. "That was the argument about the food."

"Was it?" Rhodes asked.

"Gertrude—Granny—said something about it at the ladies luncheon weeks ago. Ciran wanted to provide tacos."

"That would've been great," Rhodes said. "His taco truck is fantastic."

"We should go there too."

"Tonight?"

"No, silly." She giggled at him. "Another time. It's okay to get off the ranch more than once a year."

He rolled his eyes. "I get off the ranch more than once a year."

"Mm hm." She turned toward him. "Did you see all the plants I brought back?"

"Not yet."

He did seem to have his nose in everything at the ranch—except the homestead. "Why is that?" she asked. "You know everything that happens around the ranch. If a mouse dies in a hole out in sector eight, you know about it. And yet, you never come to the homestead to see how the yard is coming along."

He looked away from the menu, and Capri couldn't quite look him in the eye. "I don't know," he said.

"I think you do."

His name was called, and they stood up to follow the hostess back to their table. She went to get their drinks, and Capri finally got the courage to look at her boyfriend. "Why don't you want to move into the homestead?"

He blinked, gazing right back at her. "I like my cabin."

"Who says you have to live in the homestead?"

"Someone has to live there," he said. "Take care of it. It's always the ranch's owner. The oldest son."

"What if you don't have a son?"

"I don't know," he said again. "That's how it's always been in the family. Gramps ran the ranch. My dad was the oldest son, so he ran the ranch. I'm the oldest son. I'll take over the ranch in January."

Capri heard the simultaneous pride and doubt in Rhodes's voice. "And move into the homestead."

"Most likely," he said, glancing up when his glass of water came. A waiter stopped by next, and they put in their orders.

"What if the oldest son didn't want the ranch?"

"That hasn't been a problem yet," he said.

"So you want kids." It didn't come out as a question, and Capri couldn't believe she'd said it.

Rhodes nodded. "Yeah, I want kids." He lifted his water to his lips, his eyes never leaving hers. "What about you? You look like you just swallowed a beehive. You don't want kids?"

"I do," she said slowly. "I just...I'm just starting my business."

Rhodes leaned forward onto his elbows, his dark eyes practically shooting stars at her. "If we got married, Capri, you'd probably help me run the ranch."

Shock traveled through her in waves. "What?"

"That's what Granny did. That's what my mom did. They didn't have businesses." He picked up his water again. At this rate, he was going to drink the whole thing before their food even arrived.

"I—I didn't realize that was a requirement."

"It's not," he said, glancing up as the waiter put his burger and fries in front of him.

Capri tucked into her own food—the meatloaf and

mashed potatoes—because she didn't want to acknowledge that she had no idea how nor any inclination to help him run the ranch.

And that felt like a deal-breaker to her. Was it really a deal-breaker? Would he break-up with her if she insisted on keeping her landscaping company growing and open?

She didn't want to ask, because she'd just had a thing with him about working too much. So she put on a smile and listened as he told her about Jessie and Flynn, and how apparently they'd started dating three weeks ago.

"Well inside his thirty-day female fast, mind you," Rhodes said.

"Scandalous," Capri said, acting light and casual when every bite of food felt like lead in her stomach.

CHAPTER TWELVE

*R*hodes really didn't have time for another crisis on the ranch. They'd just solved their wolf problems when his bulls decided they didn't like being in their pen. He had normal ranch work to complete, and that didn't include a herd of stubborn males kicking down fences.

He arrived on the scene with a rope in his hand, though he was a terrible throw. Cami had competed in the rodeo growing up, but she'd since given it up. And she didn't have to throw ropes, but she was an excellent barrel racer.

"Where are we?" he asked Steven, the cowboy who'd first radioed him to come out to the bullpens because they "had a problem."

Rhodes was so tired of problems.

He'd been trying not to work as much, but it felt impossible. He didn't know how to do what Capri obviously wanted him to. She'd started a new contract with Roger Huntsman, and Rhodes hadn't even known until she'd been out to his place twice for yardwork.

The homestead was almost done, with just the sod coming next week—according to Capri. If there was one thing Rhodes didn't micromanage it was the homestead. His aversion to it was unsettling, but he hadn't found a way to reconcile his future with himself yet.

He had started envisioning himself living in the homestead a little bit, but only with Capri as his wife. That fantasy played out a lot as he worked around the ranch, but he hadn't said anything else to her about it.

The one time he'd brought up how his mom and grandmother had helped their husbands run the ranch, Capri had shut down quickly. That dinner was a couple of weeks old now, and Rhodes really needed to revisit the topic.

He honestly wasn't sure what Capri would do past next week, and they needed to talk about that too. The cabin was part of her compensation for the landscaping, and once that was done...she should technically move out.

"Boss?"

Rhodes blinked and shook his head. He'd missed everything Steven had just said. A headache pounded behind his eyes, and he said, "Sorry. Tell me again."

"I've got six cowboys out there, roping the bulls in. Flynn, Cami, Georgia, and Taylor almost have the fence fixed. Once we've got that secure, we just need to get the animals back in."

The situation felt under control, but Rhodes knew bulls could be unpredictable and downright dangerous. Men died from bull attacks, and he walked toward the pen to find that Georgia wasn't fixing the fence, but rather keeping watch so the others could focus on their work.

"Where's Jessie?"

"Out with the cowboys," Steven said, following him. "We have three of the ten bulls already roped."

"So they need more people out there," he said.

"I think we're situated for now," he said. "They're keeping

them out to the northeast. Away from the homestead and other animals and outbuildings."

"Good," Rhodes said, his fingers loosening on the rope he held.

"Done," Flynn called, and the four of them hurried back to Steven and Rhodes. "We can start loading 'em in, Boss."

"All right," he said, nodding to Steven. He lifted the radio to his lips and gave instructions for those who had roped bulls to bring them back.

"Start tightening the circle on the others," he said before lowering the radio. Only a few minutes later, the first bull was returned to the pen. Rhodes knew who the culprit was, and it wasn't the smaller black bull that was already back.

"Is Cyclone contained?" he asked.

"No," Steven said.

Rhodes sighed and kept watching as two, three, four, five bulls got returned to the pen. He could send out more men, but more manpower only agitated the animals, and he figured they had a system working for them. So he sat tight and waited, the minutes passing by slowly as it took longer for each bull to get roped and returned.

With eight of them in, Rhodes started to relax. Cyclone still hadn't been caught, and he nodded to Flynn. "Let's go see where the stubborn thing is." His frustration with the bull rose as he and Flynn started out with Jessie to where Cyclone had gone.

"He's edging closer and closer to the homestead," Jessie said. "I called Betsy and told her, and she spread the word to everyone there to stay out of the way."

"Mom and Dad?" Rhodes asked.

"Yep."

"Knox at the smithy?"

"He's not here today."

"Capri?"

"I'm assuming." Jessie glanced at him, her eyes worried. "Let me call Betsy again." She dug into her back pocket with her right hand, her left holding the radio. She passed it to Flynn, who walked between Rhodes and his sister, so the panicked voice coming through the speaker seemed twice as loud when Gil said, "He's charging something. Heading straight for the homestead."

Scuffling and scratching came through the line, along with Gil's labored breathing. "Oh, this is bad. Whoever's out there, call 911. Someone's down. Cyclone's angry and still on the loose. I repeat. Call for help."

"Gil," Flynn said into the radio, his eyes locked on Rhodes's. "Gil?"

"I'm going to see if I can get closer," Gil said, finally letting off the button.

"Gil," Flynn said. "Come back. Who is it?"

They'd all stopped walking, and Rhodes felt like someone had filled his veins with ice water instead of blood. "Capri?" he asked again.

Gil didn't come back, and Rhodes looked toward the homestead in the distance. If he was in a hurry, he could probably get there in five or ten minutes. And he was in a hurry.

He took off running, Jessie and Flynn calling after him. "Call for help," he yelled over his shoulder, realizing he had no radio and no way to communicate with anyone. Didn't matter. If Capri was in trouble, he had to help her.

A few minutes later, he approached the edge of the last building before he'd be out in the open, the homestead spread before him. At the corner of the shed, he paused, his heart hammering loudly in his ears.

He couldn't see a person or a bull. His phone went off, and he checked it to find Jessie had sent him a text.

Around back. Far corner from Mom's place.

Rhodes looked at the house again and still saw nothing. Deciding to make a run for it, he dashed out from the safety of the shed and headed for the huge tree in the middle of all that dirt in the yard.

The heat practically rose from the ground in waves, and Rhodes had a hard time getting a decent breath. He ducked around the fountain grasses that looked so much like the ranch land out here to the corner of the house and peered around it.

Cyclone stood about fifty feet from him, at the corner, and he was not happy. He stepped from the grass in the backyard that Capri hadn't disturbed onto the dirt where she'd re-landscaped to make sure water didn't go into his basement.

His phone sounded again, and Cyclone lifted his head. Fear struck Rhodes right between the ribs, and he pressed his back into the homestead, not caring about the heat this time. Glancing at his phone, he was able to read the message in pieces.

False alarm.

No one outside.

Get out of there.

Except now there was someone outside, and Rhodes could distinctly hear the clomping footsteps of Cyclone as he came closer, as well as the terrifying way he snorted every other moment.

Nearby, someone banged on the window, drawing his attention over his shoulder. It was Betsy, and she was gesturing for all she was worth for him to run to the front steps. Rhodes hesitated, and Betsy looked like she might come apart.

He moved, and in that moment, something loud and metallic sounded from the backyard. He ran as fast as he could toward the steps, taking them three at a time up to the porch before looking to see how close he'd come to being gored.

Cyclone wasn't there, and the front door opened. Betsy yelled, "Get in here," and slammed the door behind him after he went past her. His chest heaved as their eyes met, and he saw Capri emerge from the mud room with a pot and a wooden spoon.

Relief washed through him at the same time it ran across her face. "Okay, he's in," she said, setting the kitchenware on the island. "Let Jessie know."

Betsy's fingers flew over her phone, sending the message. "He's the only bull left."

"Maybe we should leave him until he calms down," Capri said.

Rhodes thought that was a decent idea, and he moved back to the window where Betsy had been to see if he could see Cyclone. Betsy and Capri joined him in the study—a room no one used—all of them pressing their noses against the glass.

"I hate this," Betsy said. "I should have a radio here at the homestead. Then we'd know what was going on."

"They'll get him," Rhodes said. "I have good men."

Minutes passed, and then the bull shot into the front yard, obviously angry. Capri and Betsy cried out and fell back, Rhodes with them. His adrenaline spiked, but he was utterly helpless as Cyclone started pawing the ground, not caring about Capri's careful grading and landscaping décor.

"No," he said, his voice rough around the edges. He stepped back to the window, Capri and Betsy at his side, as Cyclone proceeded to undo her weeks of hard work. He put his hand in hers and squeezed, but she didn't squeeze back.

❄

A week later, Rhodes had paid more for the yard than he'd ever wanted to. Ever. They'd gotten the bull contained, and he was now in his own pen, inside another fence. So if Cyclone got out, he still had another barrier to kick through.

Capri had not cried over her lost hard work. She'd simply gotten back to work. Rhodes admired her for that, but he was in no mood to deal with the yard.

So when he found her sitting on his front steps one night after work, a clipboard in her hands, his frustration rose as quickly as smoke from a fire.

"What now?" he asked.

"I've re-ordered a bunch of stuff," she said, "I just need a card to pay for it when I go pick it up tomorrow." She handed him a piece of paper from the clipboard, and he couldn't believe how much shrubs and decorative grasses cost.

"Do we really need all of this?"

"You approved it before."

He let the paper hang between his knees as he sat next to her. "I know. I just...I hate that yard."

She recoiled from him, and Rhodes realized what he'd said. "I mean—it's just turned out to be so expensive."

Capri swallowed, her eyes big and round. She said nothing, and Rhodes felt a chasm between them he didn't know how to cross.

"Couldn't you, I don't know. Do it cheaper?"

"Cheaper," she repeated, clearly confused. "Rhodes, it's not my fault that bull got out."

"I know that," he said, confused himself. "I just—I don't care about the yard."

"You've made that abundantly clear," she said, standing up and walking down his steps.

"It's not anything against you," he said.

"But it is, Rhodes. You walk around this ranch every day

and check on other people and their work. You never come to the homestead to see how I'm doing." She drew in a big breath, and Rhodes caught sight of the fury on her face.

"And you blame me for things that aren't my fault. You think I can do this job cheaper, when you saw the expenses months ago." She marched away from him.

"Capri," he called after her, wondering how this had gone so sideways, so fast.

CHAPTER THIRTEEN

*C*apri could not believe Rhodes was acting like the yard needing to be redone was her fault. She'd spent five full days going through the damage from that blasted bull, pulling up stomped on plants and broken bushes.

All her hard work, gone.

But hey, at least she was safe. That was her last thought each night when she went to bed, no matter how badly her back ached.

And Rhodes didn't appreciate any of it. He never had.

"I'm done," she said, stomping up her steps. "I'll move out tomorrow."

"Done?" Rhodes's voice carried to her as she went inside and slammed the door. She leaned into it, trying to breathe.

She'd barely moved from it when Rhodes knocked and then entered. "Done? Capri, you can't be done. The job isn't over yet."

"It is," she said. "You've already paid for it once, and you obviously don't want to do it again." She walked away from him and picked up one of the boxes she'd kept for when she had to move out of this cabin.

She could admit she'd been thinking about moving into the homestead with Rhodes. She'd had time to think about being a ranch owner's wife, and it was a nice thought. Especially if the cowboy playing the husband was Rhodes Quinn.

But she wouldn't be his second fiddle for her whole lifetime, constantly wondering if she was good enough for him, or if he believed in her.

Do it for cheaper.

That right there was an attitude that said he didn't know how hard she'd worked, and didn't believe she knew what she was doing.

"What are you doing?" he asked as she opened a cabinet and started putting dishes in it.

"Packing," she said, shooting him a glare. "I can't live here after the job is over, and the job is now over."

"Capri," he said, his voice weary and full of warning at the same time. "That's not what I meant."

She abandoned her packing and leaned her hip into the countertop. "What did you mean?"

He gazed at her, and Capri gave him several long seconds of time to think. He still said nothing.

"You know what I think?" she finally asked. "I think you meant exactly what you said. You don't care about the yard at the homestead. You don't want to move into the homestead, because then you'll have to admit you're in charge here but that you can't do everything. And you like doing everything."

"I've cut back on how much I work," he said, his face storming with emotion. "For you."

"No," Capri said. "You don't get to say you've done something for me, Rhodes." She went back to the box, but she honestly didn't want her cheese grater or the cereal bowls in the cupboard.

"You just told me to 'do it cheaper' when you didn't have a problem with the yard before that. You don't believe in me.

You don't think I can do this job, but you didn't want to let me know that, so you never came to the homestead to see what was happening."

"That's not true."

"It *is* true," Capri said, her tears starting to edge up her throat and burn the back of her eyes.

He didn't deny it again.

Capri's heart cracked right down the middle. It had shattered when Chase had pulled back from her. But this felt like a complete slap in the face. Rhodes taking her heart in one fist and squeezing the life out of her.

"You should go," she said, the anger inside her gone now. Now, there was only pain and humiliation. She stared down into the box, half-hoping Rhodes would stay and say something.

Instead, he said, "I don't know what to say, Capri."

She wanted to give him some Texas attitude, but she didn't have the heart. He was still fisting it, twisting the life out of it. "Nothing to say, Rhodes. I'll be gone in the morning."

"That's not necessary."

"Yes, Rhodes." She turned and faced him. "It is." She reached up into the cupboard and started putting bowls into the box. She didn't have much stuff, and she could text Betsy and ask her if she could send a couple of cowboys to her cabin in the morning to help with the bigger items.

Rhodes would be out on the ranch by five or six, and Capri paused in her packing when his boots hit the floor as he walked to the door. She watched him open the door, pause, and then leave.

The clicking of the door as it closed was the worst sound on the planet, and Capri couldn't push against the tears any longer.

THE FOLLOWING MORNING, SHE STACKED THE BOXES SHE'D packed last night and earlier that day next to the trailer. Betsy had called when Capri had texted for a couple of cowboys to come help move her out.

Capri had refused to say much about the situation, only that she needed help and she didn't want to ask Rhodes.

So just after nine, three cowboys arrived, along with Betsy, Cami, and Jessie. The women wore looks of fear and concern on their faces, and for that matter, so did the men.

"You didn't tell Rhodes," she said, looking at Betsy.

"He's in a foul mood," Jessie said, taking a quick step in front of Betsy. "I told the guys it would be a few minutes, and they snuck away."

"It's just the couch and the bed," she told them. "And these boxes." The cowboy nodded and went up the steps.

"The yard isn't finished," Cami said.

"Rhodes will take care of it," Capri said, turning to put her purse in her truck. No, she didn't have anywhere to stay that night, but she could find something. She had all day, and there was always the hotel. She'd be fine.

"Capri," Betsy said. "Why don't you just talk to him?"

"I did talk to him," Capri said. She didn't want to say anything bad about their brother, who they clearly adored. "We talked all the time, including last night." Until he walked out.

She stepped over to the sisters and embraced them in a four-way hug. "Thanks for everything." She sucked back her tears. Before she knew it, the truck was packed, and the boys had the trailer hitched to the vehicle.

It was time to go.

So she hugged the Quinn women again, got behind the

wheel, and left the ranch. Left the life she'd been enjoying in Idaho behind. Left Rhodes.

She went to the grocery store, as that seemed like a good place to start asking around for a place to rent. By lunchtime she had a few leads, and she went to the taco truck Rhodes had told her about a while ago and they'd never visited.

Over the most delicious tacos she'd ever eaten, she made a few phone calls and set up a couple of appointments to see a townhome and then a small home on the outskirts of town. She didn't need something big or even that nice. Just termite free would be great.

She sat outside, under the umbrella at the table beside the taco truck, barely aware of time passing. Before she knew it, she had to leave to get to her first appointment, and she pulled up to the address she'd been given only a couple of minutes late.

The landlord led her through the house, and Capri asked, "Any termites?"

"Termites?" the woman asked.

"I'll take it," Capri said, putting a smile on her face. Her momma had taught her to smile through the hard things and the good things, and she told herself she could survive this setback. She had another job in Quinn Valley, and she just needed a few more.

She'd be fine. She'd moved from Texas with only the hope of this job working out. She'd never told Rhodes she barely believed in herself, and she hadn't realized how much his opinion meant to her until she knew fully that he didn't think highly of her abilities.

Her chest felt like it was about to cave in on itself, but she breathed through it long enough to sign some paperwork, write a check that took her account down to two hundred and fifty dollars, and get the key to her new place.

"You're dating Rhodes Quinn, right?"

Capri looked at the woman, trying to place her. "Yes," she said, because it was easier than explaining they'd broken up twelve hours ago. "Why?"

She smiled, her hazel eyes lighting up from the inside. "Oh, my grandmother goes out to the ranch every Wednesday to meet with his." She shook her head and giggled. "She's always trying to set me up with someone. Rhodes, once, actually."

Capri put a plastic smile on her face too. "That's great. I went to the luncheon once. Who's your grandmother?"

"Nellie?"

"Oh, she's lovely," Capri said, wishing this woman would go already. She didn't want the news of her breaking up with Rhodes to get to Granny. But of course, Granny would find out eventually. Capri just wanted one day of peace, and she'd already dealt with his sisters that morning.

"Yeah, I'm the wild one," the woman said. "Zena." She laughed, and Capri joined in half-heartedly. She understood being the black sheep, and she couldn't imagine if she'd had to call Momma and tell her another boyfriend had bit the dust. Maybe she should be grateful her mother wasn't talking to her—and hadn't for months.

"Hey, do you know any of the neighbors here? Maybe someone could come help me move in my couch."

Zena tilted her head. "Rhodes isn't going to come help you?"

Annoyance flashed through Capri. She did not need Rhodes. She just needed someone with more muscles than her to get the couch and mattress inside. "He's so busy on the ranch," she said, pursing her lips. "It's okay. I'll manage."

Zena nodded down the road to the next house over. "You've got another Quinn right there. Dusty. He likes the ladies, and if you're not with Rhodes...."

Zena cleared her throat. "I'm sure he'll help you. He

works, but as soon as he sees your trailer here, I wouldn't be surprised if he came knocking on your door." Zena smiled, waved good-bye, and left Capri standing in her new house.

She looked around, her heart sinking all the way to the termite-free floor. This was not where she wanted to be today.

Surrounded by Quinns, too. This whole valley was full of them, and she *really* didn't want to stick around.

But, she hadn't wanted to spend a night in jail either, and she'd survived that. Somehow, though, this felt so much worse, and Capri sniffed, trying to keep the tears dormant.

She didn't succeed.

CHAPTER FOURTEEN

*R*hodes knew Capri had moved the moment he turned the corner and headed toward the cabins near the entrance to the ranch. The big, white trailer was gone. Her truck was gone. Everything on the ranch had felt off all day.

His sisters had avoided him, except for Georgia, who was so busy on the ranch she and Logan had purchased that she wasn't sure what was going on with everyone. He wished he wasn't sure.

In fact, he *wasn't* sure.

He didn't know what he'd done that was so awful, but his actions had shown Capri that he didn't care about the homestead project.

And he hadn't. It had stressed him too much. Didn't that mean he trusted her *more*, not less?

He wasn't sure, and he'd been thinking about it all dang day. As he approached the row of cabins, Granny came out of hers. "Dinner with us, Rhodes?" she called, and Rhodes wanted to decline. But he hadn't seen his grandparents as much as he normally did, and he continued past his place to theirs.

"Evening, Granny," he said, stepping past her and into the house. It smelled like roast beef, and Rhodes's mouth started to water.

"Harley, get the ice cream out," she said. "Then it can soften while we eat."

Rhodes washed his hands while his grandfather got out the ice cream and Granny lifted the lid on a pot on the stove. "Okay," she said. "Everything's ready."

Rhodes said grace at his grandfather's request and he loaded his plate with meat, potatoes, gravy, and Granny's cheddar-covered broccoli before sitting down.

"Is Cyclone behaving?" Gramps asked, and Rhodes nodded while he chewed.

"The better question is whether Rhodes is behaving," Granny said, cutting her meat with a knife and fork.

"Oh, leave the boy be," Gramps said.

"I will not leave him be," Granny said, her bright blue eyes sharp as nails. "And he's not a boy. The man is thirty-six years old, and not getting any younger to have a family."

"Granny," Rhodes said, reaching for his glass of water. "Capri broke up with me."

"Oh, I know all about it," Granny said, waving her hand. "Watched her drive away from here." She clucked her tongue like that was the worst thing on the planet. "She didn't even finish the homestead. It's a mess."

Rhodes hadn't been by to look at it. He couldn't. His heart felt like it was dangling in his chest by a thin string and seeing the state of the yard at the homestead would sever that.

Capri had cancelled the sod while she cleaned up after Cyclone's damage, and Rhodes really could leave the lawn exactly how it was. Bare dirt. Who cared anyway? No one came out to the ranch except family and co-workers. He wouldn't be entertaining there.

Rhodes said nothing—he was exceptionally good at that. Gramps didn't either, and Rhodes felt a connection to his grandfather in that moment that he'd overlooked before. Their eyes met a couple of times while Granny talked about the house Capri had rented from one of Nellie's grandchildren, and blah blah blah.

Rhodes didn't care. Or maybe he did. Of course he wanted a wife and family, someone to take over the ranch when he got older. But Betsy and Georgia both had fiancés now, and perhaps one of their children could take over.

He didn't know, and he was so tired. He stayed for ice cream, kissed his grandparents, and went home. It felt odd that the other two cabins beside him were empty, though Capri had only been there for a couple of months.

"Almost three," he muttered to himself, wishing the mechanic he'd hired had needed the cabin. But Jonas had a place in town and just drove out to the ranch the way Knox did when he came to the smithy.

Rhodes had just kicked his boots off when his phone buzzed. From his father: *We need to talk about the winter feed.*

Rhodes scowled at his phone. The winter feed? It was mid-July.

When? he texted back. He was in the middle of saying when he could come over the next couple of days when his father said, *Come now.*

Rhodes didn't want to go now. He wanted to lie on the couch and fall asleep so he wouldn't have to think about Capri's cabin being empty. About her being gone. About not seeing her anymore, since he didn't get to town all that often.

In the end, his dad wouldn't leave it alone, and Rhodes stuffed his feet back in his boots and drove down the road to the homestead. He couldn't get to his parents' house in the back without seeing the yard.

And, wow, what a huge mess. Capri surely had some method to her madness, but Rhodes would never figure it out. The evening wind kicked up, taking some of the dirt from the expansive lawn with it.

Rhodes sat in his truck for a few minutes, just looking at the torn-up yard. Betsy wouldn't be happy, though she'd been over at Knox's house, tending to his yard—hers by Christmas. So really, it was just Rhodes left to deal with the empty flower beds, the neatly sloped ground that should be covered with grass, the way the trees looked forlorn now instead of majestic and beautiful.

He got out of his truck and walked onto the bare dirt. At least it seemed to all be in the place it was supposed to be in. There weren't piles or holes or anything like that. The earth was hard-packed and brown, and Rhodes knew he didn't want to live with a yard like that.

Cyclone wasn't Capri's fault, Rhodes knew that. His reluctance to become the boss and move into the homestead wasn't her fault either.

He picked up a shovel that leaned against the tree and glanced around. This yard needed a lot of work to get it looking good again. He pulled out his phone and saw that his father had texted a couple more times. Rhodes hadn't even heard his phone go off.

Searching quickly, he pulled up the nursery in Lewiston that Capri had ordered from. "Hey, yeah," he said. "It's Rhodes Quinn. I believe I had an order up there I was supposed to pick up today?"

"Let me see," the woman said. "That order was canceled, sir."

"How hard would it be to put it back in?" He turned in a slow circle as the woman checked.

"I could have it ready next Tuesday," she said.

Five days. Rhodes could wait five more days. "Please order it for me," he said. "I'll be there on Tuesday to pick it up."

Then he'd fix up this yard just the way Capri had planned, and he'd get her back out here and apologize, apologize, apologize until she accepted it. Accepted him, just the way he was.

He didn't want to think about what might happen if she didn't do that. If she couldn't handle the way he worked, or flat-out didn't want to be the ranch owner's wife.

His heart stuttered in his chest as voices came through the front door. "See?" Betsy said. "His truck's here." She came out onto the porch with their dad. "He's right there, Dad."

Rhodes didn't move, his grip on the shovel sure. "I need to get this yard done, don't I?"

"Your mother would appreciate it," his dad said. "She worked hard on this yard for a lot of years."

Rhodes looked at his father, who came down the steps and joined him on the bare dirt. "What's going on with you?" he asked.

"I'm nervous about taking over the ranch," Rhodes said, looking his father right in the eye. "I can't be you, and I'm afraid it's all going to fall apart." The worries and doubts that had been accumulating the past few months streamed from him, and one of them was a concern about how his father would view him if Rhodes admitted to being afraid.

"I don't want to live here alone," he said, gesturing to the big house. "I don't have a wife. I don't even have a girlfriend anymore. No family." Rhodes bit back the rest of his troubles and looked away from his dad. "I'm not ready, Dad." He ducked his head and studied the dust on their boots.

He wasn't sure what his father would do. Maybe a lecture, as he'd gotten exceptionally good at those over the years. Maybe just the silence between them would be enough.

Rhodes didn't expect his father to hug him and give him a few healthy pats on the back. "I felt the exact same way, son. You're doin' just fine." He held him tight, and Rhodes held onto his father too.

"What if I mess up?"

"You will," his dad said. "But you can't break the ranch, Rhodes. Trust me, if it were possible, I'd have done it." He stepped back and held his son at arm's length, his eyes boring right into Rhodes's. "Okay? You'll make mistakes—one of which is letting that pretty blonde out of your sight—but you can fix them. You've got the support of your family, and all of your people on this ranch. Everyone wants to succeed. Everything will be fine."

Rhodes nodded. "Okay, Dad."

"Okay." He dropped his hands and looked around the yard. "We do need to get this cleaned up though."

"I'm going to finish it," Rhodes said. "Surprise that pretty blonde and try to get her back."

"Oh, I like the way you're thinking." His dad smiled. "Now, which do you think is going to be harder? This landscaping or your love life?"

Rhodes burst out laughing. "Honestly, Dad, I think it's a draw."

"Your mother and I will start praying for the love life." He slung his arm around Rhodes's shoulders. "Again."

Now, *that* was a good idea, and Rhodes sent a prayer heavenward that his attempts at landscaping for Capri wouldn't make things worse.

CHAPTER FIFTEEN

apri had little success drumming up more business. It seemed like Quinn Valley residents didn't mind mowing their own lawns, or they already had a lawn service, or they didn't need a new retaining wall or fountain feature in their yards.

Which was actually great, because Capri didn't really know how to do a retaining wall or fountain feature anyway.

She'd lived in the little house on Bedford Street for four days before she admitted to herself that she'd have to get a job if she wanted to pay rent in August. Even then, she might be cutting it close.

Zena had given her permission to work in the yard at the house, and Tuesday morning found her puttering around in the rose bushes. The house had several, from pink lemonade to deep burgundy to tangerine.

Capri loved roses, and she'd already determined she would have lots of rose bushes edging her house. Thoughts of where that house should be, and what jobs she might be qualified for in Quinn Valley ran through her mind. She really needed to start applying today.

So she finished clipping back the roses and went inside to get online. She'd worked as a trainer and receptionist at a boarding stable in Crescent Lake. She'd been a substitute teacher. She'd waited tables at one of the most popular steak-houses in Hill Country.

But most of the jobs in Quinn Valley were for manual labor. Construction. There were three secretarial jobs, and she filled out online applications for those. And the grocery store was hiring.

Capri pressed her eyes closed, praying she didn't have to apply there. She could only imagine the questions that would raise, and how she'd have to explain to everyone who she was, why she'd come to Quinn Valley, and why things with Rhodes just hadn't worked out.

She hadn't heard from him, not once, since their argument and break-up the week prior. Almost seven days....

She didn't want to admit that his lack of communication hurt, but it did. Capri thought he might have fought for her, for them.

With the job applications filled out, Capri turned her attention to making herself something to eat. She could live like a college student if she had to, and she pulled out a can of soup and a couple of pieces of bread.

Someone knocked on the door, and she turned that way, a little confused. Yes, Dusty had come to help her move in her heavy items. Other than that, Capri had not met anyone else in town. She'd skipped church for fear of seeing Rhodes, and she wasn't sure she was in the mood to meet someone tonight.

They knocked again, though, and Capri's adrenaline spiked. She crossed through the house to open the door, pausing to look through the peephole first.

She gasped and almost fell backward at the squinty sight of Rhodes Quinn standing on her front porch.

Drawing in a deep breath, she pressed one hand over her heart to feel it jackhammering against her palm. "Be calm," she whispered to herself as she pulled her hair from the messy bun it was in from that morning's yard work.

"Capri," he called, knocking again, longer this time. So he wasn't giving up.

Capri's hopes soared, but she shoved them back down inside herself, straightened her shirt, and pulled open the door. "Hello, Rhodes."

He simply stared at her, his eyes traveling down the length of her body and back.

"Can I help you?" she asked, her Texas manners making an appearance.

He flinched as if she'd hit him square in the face with ice water. "Yes," he said. "As a matter of fact, you can." He hooked his thumb over his shoulder to the truck parked behind hers. "I went and got all those plants you ordered from the nursery in Lewiston. I need you to come help me put them in right."

Capri heard him. She knew he'd spoken English, but she was having trouble getting the words to mean the right thing.

A handsome, sexy grin touched his lips. "I can't find your garden map, and I can't do the landscaping without you." He reached out, his fingertips barely brushing hers. "Please forgive me, Capri. I was going to finish the yard and then lure you out the ranch somehow to apologize. But I can't seem to do anything without you. I can't even enjoy ice cream."

Capri couldn't help smiling as she shook her head.

"I work too much," he said. "I'm working—ha ha. Get it? Working?"

She didn't laugh, and neither did he. He cleared his throat and continued with, "I'm working on cutting down my hours. I'm working on accepting that I have to move into that homestead by myself, though I hate the very idea."

He inched closer to her, lacing his fingers through hers now. "I want to work on our relationship too." He looked right into her eyes, and Capri lost herself in the dark depths of his. "I love you, Capri Haywood, and I need you on that ranch with me."

I love you, Capri.

She stared back at him, all her synapses firing like crazy now.

"Please," he said again. "Please forgive me. And please say something."

Capri suddenly understood why he needed so much time to organize his thoughts into sentences. She blinked at him. "I have the garden map in my purse," she said. "I'll be right back."

She left the door open so he could come in if he chose to, but he stayed on the porch while she grabbed her purse. Back in the doorway, she pulled the paper out and extended it toward him.

He didn't take it. "You have to come with it," he said. "I want us to do it together."

"The landscaping?" she asked.

"Everything," he said, his voice husky and hoarse. "I trust you, sweetheart. I don't want to do this without you and have it be wrong."

"I'm sure it wouldn't be wrong."

"It will absolutely be wrong." Rhodes sighed, clearly frustrated. "Everything's been wrong since you left."

Capri looked at Rhodes, heard all the things he was saying. She tucked the map back into her purse and went out onto the porch with him. "All right, Rhodes. I'll come."

His eyes crinkled as he smiled. "Does that mean...? Well, what does that mean?"

Capri put her palm over his pulse this time, enjoying the

way it thumped steadily against her skin. "It means I forgive you, and I love you too."

His eyes widened, and then he swept one arm around her, using the other to pull his hat off his head. He leaned down and kissed her, a new kind of urgency and edge to his touch she hadn't experienced before.

"I'm sorry," he whispered.

"I know."

He touched his mouth to her jaw. "I love you."

"I heard you the first time." Capri smiled and giggled, glad with every fiber of her being for this cowboy in her life. "I've been pretty miserable without you, too."

"Oh, yeah?"

"Yeah. I had to apply for all kinds of jobs today. Turns out, not many people need a landscape architect in Quinn Valley." She led him down her steps and to his truck, where she positioned herself right next to him for the drive out to the ranch.

"I know I mentioned it once, but you reacted poorly. What about helping me run the ranch?"

"Oh, I can't do that," she said. "That's for the ranch owner's *wife*." She looked at him and raised her eyebrows.

"Capri, I'd marry you tomorrow," he said, backing out of her driveway and setting them on the road toward the ranch.

A bolt of lightning struck her. "Really?"

He reached over and slipped his hand into hers. "I really don't want to move into that homestead by myself."

"Doesn't sound like a good reason to get married," she said. "What if you can't stand me after a few months?"

"I think that's impossible," he said.

"I'm bossy," she said. "Opinionated. Unemployed. And I don't want you working sixteen hours a day."

"I'm aware," he said, making a right turn when he

should've gone left. "I feel like ice cream tonight. What's your favorite today?"

Capri burst out laughing, and the best sound in the world was Rhodes joining in.

AFTER THEY'D STOPPED FOR ICE CREAM—MINT CHOCOLATE chip and cookies and cream—Rhodes did finally drive them out to the ranch. He pulled up to the edge of the lawn at the homestead and got out, the bag with the ice cream already in his hand.

"I'm going to run this inside," he said, jogging up the sidewalk and going up the steps to the house. Capri got out of the truck and moved around to the back.

It sure seemed like everything she'd ordered was there, and she opened the tailgate and started unloading it all.

Rhodes returned quickly and helped her, putting shrubs in their containers where she told him to.

Working together, they got everything in and planted in a relatively short amount of time. She stepped back as the last container of fountain grass went in, and Rhodes joined her.

"My dad asked me which would be harder, the landscaping or my love life."

Capri snuggled into his side as he slung his arm around her waist. "What did you tell him?"

"I think it's kind of both," Rhodes said. "We'll have to constantly be landscaping our love, don't you think?" He bent down and touched his lips to her forehead. "Like, right now, it's new and exciting and I want to come out and watch the shrubs grow. You know?"

Capri smiled. "Yeah, I know."

"But in a year, it might need some work. Some old stuff

ripped out, and some new stuff put in. Fertilizer and someone to care about it."

She glanced up at him. "So the landscaping is like your love life."

"They're both pretty hard," he said. "And I know I said I didn't care about the yard, but that's not true. I do care about it. I care about it a lot. I just...wasn't in a good place."

"I know," Capri said, lifting up onto her toes to kiss him. "I know."

CHAPTER SIXTEEN

*R*hodes was grateful for the power of forgiveness, and the fact that Capri was mature enough to talk through things with him.

With the yard done, the homestead became a beautiful place, looking almost like the wildness of the ranch went right up to the front door.

Over the past month since he and Capri had finished the yard together, he'd been going over to his grandparents' house like he had before he'd started dating Capri. He didn't miss picking up Granny from her hair appointments, and he ate dinner with them a few times a week.

Capri came too, and she often brought fruit, meat, and dairy products from the grocery store that were about to expire. Gramps was in pure heaven with all the ice cream, but Rhodes could see why it had been on the shelf and not been bought. After all, who wanted to eat dairy-free, gluten-free soy ice cream?

His grandfather, who claimed the double chocolate was delicious. Rhodes only shook his head and smiled when Gramps tried to get him to eat the stuff.

He'd been meeting with his father a lot more too, and he wiped his boots on their front mat before knocking on their door. "Dad?" he called as he went in without waiting for either of his parents to answer.

This house was four times as big as his cabin, and he paused in the doorway, realizing he'd live here too. In thirty or forty years, this would be his house. Because his father had gotten married so young, he'd needed somewhere for Gramps and Granny to live, and thus, the four cabins lining the road on the way into the ranch had been built. But in thirty or forty years, his parents would most likely be gone. His dad had turned sixty-one this past spring, and by the time Rhodes was ready to retire, he'd be in his nineties.

"Dad?" he called again, but no one answered. Rhodes went into the kitchen and got out a bottle of water. His dad would be back soon, and then Rhodes could ask him all the questions he wanted.

The weekly sessions had morphed from his father lecturing him about water rights and animal care, to how to be a good boss and still have a role in the family. These were the lessons Rhodes desperately needed, and they'd brought him closer to his parents.

"He's here," his mom said as the front door opened. "Sorry, Rhodes. We went over to see Libby and Randall."

"It's fine," Rhodes said, giving his mom a hug. "How are they doing?" He didn't get to see his aunt and uncle much, except at the family functions.

"Great. We were just catching up." His mother flashed a smile, and Rhodes hoped he had good sibling relationships with his sisters like his parents did when he got older.

His dad came in, carrying a couple of brown bags of groceries. "Saw Capri at the store. She said to say hi." He grinned at Rhodes. "When are you going to ask her to marry you?"

"Harvey," his mom said, and she looked at Rhodes with compassion in her eyes. "You take your time, honey."

"I was actually thinking of doing it this weekend," Rhodes admitted. "They're having that huge tent sale at the grocery store, and I talked to Flynn and Newt, and they're willing to help me out."

"With what?" His dad looked perplexed. "Don't you just ask them these days?"

"No, Dad." Rhodes smiled at him. "It has to be a big thing. Didn't you know?"

"Oh, he doesn't watch the Internet videos," his mom said, moving into the kitchen to unpack the groceries they'd bought. "But very exciting, you asking Capri to marry you."

"You don't think it's too fast?"

"Rhodes, you don't do anything fast," his dad said. "It's fine."

Rhodes tried not to be offended by what his father had said. He made some quick decisions, but no, he didn't think who he was going to spend the rest of his life with should be a decision he made overnight.

"Mom?" he asked. "Three weddings, right on top of each other?"

"Well, Georgia isn't until November," she said.

"Mom, it's almost September," he said. "You're talking less than three months."

Her hands stilled with a can of tomato soup in each one. "Is that right?"

"Yes," he and his father said together.

"Oh, my goodness," she said. "I better figure out what's going on with her."

"And Betsy is at Christmas," Rhodes said, thinking no matter how he sliced it, he was going to have to move into the homestead by himself. He couldn't upstage his sisters, and Capri would need time to plan a wedding. Wouldn't she?

They'd talked a little about it, but not much. He wondered if her mother would come, and he sure hoped so. Adding that to his prayer list, he focused back on his parents.

"Maybe spring? I'll see what Capri says. She might not even say yes."

"She'll say yes," his mother said, adding the roll of her eyes to the statement. "Which brings us to today's meeting. You wanted to know if I'd be willing to talk to Capri about being a rancher's wife."

"Yes," he said. "She's expressed some anxiety over that, and I told her I'd ask you."

"She's friendly with Granny, isn't she?"

"Yeah, but I think they spend their time talking about other people." Rhodes shook his head. "I don't get it, but they seem to love to pontificate about who's seeing who, and who might be pregnant yet."

"My mother is a special woman," his dad said with a smile. "Gotta love her."

"She has a heart of gold," Rhodes's mother said, and he couldn't disagree.

"Anyway, could you?"

"Of course," his mother said. "Should I invite her to lunch?"

"Sure. She has a weird schedule."

"I have no schedule," his mom said. "I'll text her."

His dad came out of the kitchen and nodded toward the office. Rhodes started to follow him, the plastic water bottle crinkling as he tightened his grip on it. He wasn't sure what his dad was going to say today, but it didn't matter.

It would be good advice, and Rhodes needed to hear it.

❄

"THERE ARE SO MANY PEOPLE HERE," HE COMPLAINED LATER that week. The white tent in the parking lot of the grocery store covered at least half of the stalls. Cars filled the other half, with more trying to come in.

"This is insane," Flynn agreed.

"Come on," Jessie said. "She'll be off in an hour, and we don't have much time to build this thing."

Rhodes followed his sister, the air becoming cooler as they moved under the tent. The grocery store in Quinn Valley was famous for its soda box display in front of both entrances. They did a Superbowl theme in February, video game designs for kids, Santa going down the chimney in the winter, all of it.

And since Rhodes had grown up with the owner of the store, he'd called in a favor. Capri would probably laugh at that, because she'd once accused him of knowing everyone in town—and he kind of did.

If he didn't personally, he had a family member or childhood friend who could put him in touch with the right person.

So it was that he found himself with Flynn, Jessie, Cami, Newt, Clay, Betsy, and Knox in front of at least five hundred soda boxes. "Oh, boy," Rhodes said, taking off his hat and reseating it as Marshall approached.

"There you go," he said. "Do you want to text me when you finish? That way, I can keep Capri from going on break until you're ready."

"Yes," Rhodes said. "And thanks, Marshall. This is going to be great." At least he hoped so. He'd wanted to put the whole saying in soda boxes, but it was too long. *Will you marry me?* Took up a lot of space, and he pulled the sketch out of his back pocket.

"Okay, guys," he said, though it was not the first time any of them had seen the sketch. "Let's do this."

SEVENTY-FIVE MINUTES LATER, HIS NERVES FIRED EVERY other second. The display was built. His friends and family had fanned out, and Jessie was going to record the proposal from behind the corner of the soda boxes.

Capri was on her way.

Rhodes slicked his palms down the front of his jeans and checked to make sure the ring box still perched on the box of diet cola nearest him. It did, because he'd literally set it there two minutes ago.

He swallowed and glanced around. Where was she? Marshall had said he'd sent her Rhodes's way five minutes ago.

All at once, she appeared in front of him, wearing jeans, her grocery store T-shirt, and her hair in a high ponytail. She was the most gorgeous woman he'd ever met.

She sucked in a breath, her eyes widening as she scanned the display behind him. Over the course of the six weeks she'd worked here, she'd complained about having to set up the soda box displays more than once.

They definitely weren't her favorite. Now that Rhodes had done one, he understood why.

"Capri," he said, moving forward. He got down on one knee, obviously not wasting any time. The ground was hot despite the tent and dug into his knee. "I love you. Shoot. Just a sec."

He ran back to the boxes and grabbed the most important one—the one with the diamond inside. He returned to her, glad she was smiling now. "I mean, the boxes pretty much spell it out," he said, staying on both feet this time. "But I love you, and I want to marry you, and I'm wondering...will you marry me?"

The boxes behind him spelled out *Marry me?* in all capital

letters, the boxes white against a variety of darker red ones. Jessie had managed to find yellow boxes too, to make a ring, and Flynn had made sure the diamond was done in white boxes as well.

It was pretty much the perfect display for a marriage proposal, and Rhodes glanced over his shoulder at it again.

Capri's hands touched either side of his face, guiding his attention back to her. "This is wonderful," she said, tears filling her eyes. They also held nothing but love and hope and Rhodes felt that same way. Like the whole future was in front of them, and they could conquer it—only if they were together.

"I love you," he said again.

"Show her the ring," Jessie called, and Rhodes chuckled, his fingers slipping on the box a little bit.

He opened the ring box. "If you hate it, we can go get a different one. This is actually Granny's setting, and I had it cleaned up real nice for you."

"Her ring?" Capri looked from the box to Rhodes. "Really?"

"One of them," he said. "Granny's kind of spoiled."

Capri giggled and threw her arms around Rhodes. "I love it. I love you." She kissed him, and Rhodes didn't really want that on the video. But he sure did like kissing Capri, so he focused on that.

"You haven't said yes," he whispered against her lips.

She pulled back, a huge smile on her face. "Yes, I'll marry you."

Relief swam through his system, and his fingers didn't shake as he slid the ring on her finger. They faced the soda display together, and he said, "I see what you hate about these."

She just laughed, and everyone who'd been watching came over to congratulate them. Jessie made them stand by the display while she took a million pictures, but Rhodes didn't mind.

He was in love, and the woman had said yes. He knew they'd be able to landscape their lives into whatever they needed to, and he'd never been happier.

Read on for a sneak peek of the next book in the Quinn Valley Ranch Romance series, **BIRTHDAY BOYFRIEND! Then go read it in paperback.**

And keep reading to get the coveted Quinn family recipe for Mint Chocolate Chip Ice Cream!

MINT CHOCOLATE CHIP ICE CREAM

Mint Chocolate Chip Ice Cream

*I*ngredients:

3 cups of fresh spearmint leaves (not stems), rinsed, drained, packed

1 cup milk

2 cups heavy cream (divided, 1 cup and 1 cup)

2/3 cup sugar

A pinch of salt

6 egg yolks

6 ounces semisweet chocolate or dark chocolate, chopped fine, keep in the freezer until used

STEP-BY-STEP INSTRUCTIONS:

1. Steep the mint leaves in cream and milk: Put the mint leaves in a heavy saucepan with the 1 cup of milk and 1 cup of the cream. Heat until just steaming (do not let boil), remove from heat, cover, and let stand for 30 minutes. Reheat the

mixture until steaming, remove from heat and let stand for 15 more minutes.

2. Chill remaining cream in an ice bath: While the mint is infusing in step 1, prepare the remaining cream over an ice bath. Pour the remaining 1 cup of cream into a medium size metal bowl, set in ice water (with lots of ice) over a larger bowl. Set a mesh strainer on top of the bowls. Set aside.

3. Strain out the mint leaves, add sugar: Strain the milk cream mixture into a separate bowl, pressing against the mint leaves with a rubber spatula in a sieve to get the most liquid out of them. Return the milk cream mixture to the saucepan. Add sugar and salt to the mixture. Heat until just steaming again, stirring until sugar has dissolved. Remove from heat.

4. Temper the egg yolks with hot milk cream: Whisk the egg yolks in a medium sized bowl. Slowly pour the heated milk cream mixture into the egg yolks, whisking constantly so that the egg yolks are tempered by the warm mixture, but not cooked by it. Scrape the warmed egg yolks back into the saucepan.

5. Heat until mixture begins to thicken: Return the saucepan to the stove, stirring the mixture constantly over medium heat with a wooden spoon, scraping the bottom as you stir, until the mixture thickens and coats the spoon so that you can run your finger across the coating and have the coating not run. This can take about 10 minutes.

6. Strain custard mixture into cream in ice bath: Pour the custard through the strainer (from step 2) and stir into the cold cream to stop the cooking.

7. Chill completely: Chill the mixture thoroughly in the refrigerator (at least a couple of hours) or stir the mixture in the bowl placed over the ice bath until thoroughly chilled (20 minutes or so).

8. Process in ice cream maker: Process the mixture in your

ice cream maker according to the manufacturer's instructions.

9. Add chopped chocolate: Once the ice cream has been made in the ice cream maker it should be pretty soft. Gently fold in the finely chopped chocolate.

10. Chill in freezer: Put in an airtight container and place in the freezer for at least an hour, preferably several hours. If it has been frozen for more than a day, you may need to let it sit at room temperature for a few minutes to soften it before serving.

**RECIPE FROM SIMPLY RECIPES

SNEAK PEEK! BIRTHDAY BOYFRIEND CHAPTER ONE:

"Granny?" Jessica Quinn pushed open the front door of her grandmother's cottage at the same time she called her name.

The house smelled delicious, like salted cured meats and yeast—which could only mean one thing. Kolaches.

Her granny was famous for her sausage kolaches, and Jessie could only hope she could eat one now *and* at poker night later.

"Betsy said you'd have something for me tonight," she said, feeling weary from head to toe. Perhaps she shouldn't have agreed to take her sister's place at the monthly poker night.

Betsy usually played the cards with a few cowboys here at Quinn Valley Ranch, but since she and Knox had become more serious, she'd been getting subs for her poker games. Jessie had said no a couple of times now, because she knew who Betsy played with.

And she didn't need to make a bigger fool of herself in front of Flynn Hollister. The man was her brother's right-hand-man and most trusted cowboy. And a complete player.

Well, not really, but he sure did have a lot of ladies falling all over him all the time.

"Hello, dear," Granny said as she turned from the stove. She'd been brushing an egg wash on a sheet pan of unbaked kolaches, and they were the most beautiful sight Jessie had ever seen. "I'm running a bit behind. Can I bring these down to you when they're done?"

"Oh, you don't have to do that," Jessie said. "I can swing back this way and get them."

"Pish posh," Granny said. "I'll do it. Betsy said you just needed them by seven."

Honestly, Jessie had no idea what time it was. She needed a shower and a nap, and she could only have one at the expense of the other. "Yeah," she said.

"So I'll bring them down. You go ahead and go get yourself all dolled up."

Jessie laughed and took a foil-wrapped chocolate from the bowl on Granny's counter. Her grandmother always had something good to eat in that bowl, and Jessie really needed a sweet right now.

"It's nothing to get dolled up for," she told Granny.

"Betsy said there would be cowboys there." Granny smiled at her, those bright blue eyes sparkling with mischief. Jessie had seen this look before, and she didn't like it. Not one little bit.

"Yeah, Granny," she said dryly. "All the same cowboys I see around the ranch every day." She shook her head. "Trust me, no one to impress."

"Oh, there's someone," Granny said as if she could work magic and produce a cowboy that would look at Jessie and see the woman she was. "You just listen to Granny and go get ready. I'll bring these by later."

Jessie took another chocolate as she chuckled. "All right,

Grams. Thanks so much." On her way out the front door, she sent a quick message to Betsy.

You owe Granny. Did you know she's making kolaches?

She said she wanted to, Betsy sent back. *Said it was a special night for you, and you needed the power of the Quinn kolaches.*

Jessie had no idea what that meant, but she knew Granny had a funny way of trying to set up her grandchildren. This couldn't be that—it was only kolaches. And Betsy brought food to all the poker games.

Bringing something to share was part of the rules. Everyone looked forward to Betsy's culinary creations, so they'd already be disappointed when Jessie walked in instead of her sister. Thankfully, Jessie would have the kolaches, and she suddenly wondered if they did hold some power she didn't know about.

Once at the homestead, Jessie showered and shaved her legs and then got busy curling her hair in the basement bathroom, hoping with everything she had that Cami wouldn't come downstairs. Then she wouldn't have to explain anything to her little sister.

She could sneak out the glass doors down here, and no one would have to know she'd dolled herself up as if she were going to church to go to...poker night out in the east barn.

Flynn hadn't had a girlfriend for about a week now, and Jessie thought tonight was as good of a night as any to show him he didn't have to go into the dance hall to find his next date. She was right there in front of him, working alongside him every day out on the ranch.

Not that Flynn ever had to look very hard for a willing female to hold his hand or spend time at his side.

"It's no wonder," Jessie muttered to herself as she swept mascara on her eyelashes. The man was drop-dead gorgeous, and she may or may not have had a huge crush on him for the past year.

And he was so *Flynn* that he hadn't even noticed her attempts at flirting. Or she was just really bad at it. Either way, she hadn't been on a date in a really long time. Most men slid their attention right past her to Cami, the more feminine sister, the one with more blonde in her hair than red, the one who wore pumps while Jessie wore cowgirl boots.

Grabbing her phone, she quickly texted Betsy. *You didn't tell them I was coming, did you?*

Of course not, Betsy sent back. *If I had, they'd all cancel.*

Jessie frowned at the message, not sure if she should take it as a compliment or not. It wasn't her fault she was extraordinarily gifted at games, especially card games that required her to read another person.

It also wasn't her fault she worked her father's ranch with her brother and all the cowboys so that she had better biceps than most women. She'd learned, though, that a lot of men found her intimidating, and she attributed that to her lack of male interest.

And Granny said she brought over the kolaches. They're sitting on the upstairs kitchen counter.

Jessie groaned, because now she had to go upstairs. Cami would surely see her then, and she'd be late to poker night. She didn't want to be late. She actually wanted to be early, so she could lean against the chicken coop in the distance and watch Flynn enter the barn.

She pushed the thought away. She wasn't a creeper. She just had a crush. *An insane crush,* she told herself, as Flynn had always viewed her and treated her like a little sister. And yet, the hope inside her wailed with strength, and she hadn't been able to let go of the fantasy of the two of them together.

After glossing her lips with a wand of peach delight, she pulled on her cowgirl boots and checked her T-shirt. It wasn't as manly as the plaid shirts she wore to work in, and she'd decided she could try to make Flynn realize she was a woman and not just another one of the guys. The pink shirt clung to her curves and the word COWGIRL was spelled out in black letters across her chest.

He could read, she knew that. She wondered if he'd even look at her at all tonight. Invisibility seemed to be another of Jessie's specialties, and she actually prayed for the superpower as she crept upstairs to get the snack Granny had left for her.

"Still warm," she said around the sweet dough and spicy sausage. She'd just turned to escape out the back door when Cami came through it. She paused, taking in Jessie's curled hair and sliding her eyes down to her best cowgirl boots.

"Where are you going?" Her eyes widened as she pulled in a breath. "Oh, my stars. Do you have a date?"

Not yet, she thought as she scoffed for her sister's benefit. "No, of course not. Poker night."

Cami's eyes narrowed. "Poker night? You look like you're going out with the hottest man in town." She reached out and gripped Jessie's forearm. "Just tell me who he is."

"He's no one," Jessie said, already frustrated with the questions. Betsy, Cami, and Georgia had been trying to get Jessie to say who she had a crush on for months now. It wasn't happening. The Quinns weren't exactly known for their secret-keeping abilities, and while she loved her sisters, she didn't trust that one of them wouldn't accidentally say something to someone.

And before she knew it, Flynn would know about her crush and she'd never get the opportunity to go out with him.

She looked down at the kolaches, actually praying for whatever power Granny thought they had. "I'm going to be late," she said. "Don't wait up for me."

"Hey, just a sec," Cami said as Jessie breezed by her. "Mom wanted me to double-check and make sure you're free tomorrow night."

"For what?"

"For your birthday," Cami said, shaking her head as she smiled. "I swear, Jess, you're the only person who doesn't remember their own birthday."

"I am not," she said, though she couldn't say she was overly excited about turning thirty. Maybe if she had a boyfriend to kiss her and bring her flowers, sure. But tomorrow would just be another day, with calves to feed and hay to mow and Flynn to admire. "Tomorrow's fine," she said.

"No hot dates?"

"Nope," she said, escaping out the door and practically flying down the steps to the blue and white ranch truck she used. She didn't actually own her own car. Or a house. Or much of anything.

When Rhodes took over the ranch, he'd move from the cabin beside Gramps and Granny to the homestead. She and Cami still lived there, and so would Betsy and Georgia until they got married and moved out. She wasn't entirely sure of their plans, but she knew Rhodes would let her stay in the homestead as long as she wanted.

Honestly, she wanted to just trade places with him. He could have the homestead; she'd take his cabin.

Her heart started beating faster and faster the closer she got to the east barn. By the time she got out of the truck and collected the tray of kolaches, her pulse sprinted through her chest. She managed to walk to the doors and open them to find the atmosphere lively and charged, with a round table set up for poker and a long one holding the food.

"Jessie?" Newt asked, and it was as if everything came screeching to a halt. All the conversation. All the laughter. All the eating.

"Hello, boys," she said, adding a sway to her hips as she walked toward the food table. "Betsy needed a sub, and so here I am."

A collective groan went up, but Jessie just smiled around at each of them. Newt. Clay. Wyatt.

And Flynn.

Her heartbeat fluttered now, especially when he stepped forward and asked, "Are these the famous Quinn kolaches?"

"Mm hmm," she said, taking in a deep breath of that sexy cologne and trying not to swoon at his nearness. His dark eyes looked from the tray of food she carried to her eyes, and she dove right on in and started swimming around.

It was dangerous in those depths, but she didn't care.

Tonight, she felt lucky.

After all, she had the kolaches—and all of Flynn Hollister's attention.

You can read <u>BIRTHDAY BOYFRIEND</u> in paperback right now!

Contracted Cowboy (Book 1): A fake ad brings a cowboy to Georgia's door just in time for all the Quinn family holiday parties, so she hires Logan to be her boyfriend. Nothing can go wrong with this plan...except she might lose her heart to her newly contracted cowboy.

Secret Sweetheart (Book 2):
She's a domestic goddess. He works on her father's ranch. They could have forever...if they could take their relationship out of the shadows. **Can she overcome her anxiety and fear and build a life with Knox? Or will their relationship be doomed to die in the shadows at Quinn Valley Ranch?**

Landscaping Love (Book 3): He hired her to landscape the yard, but she's going to make him re-evaluate who he lets into his heart. **Can Rhodes and Capri landscape their love? Or will they go their separate ways once the yard is finished?**

Birthday Boyfriend (Book 4): This Quinn cowgirl doesn't need a lot for her birthday...just the cowboy she's been crushing on for months. Will Flynn ever see Jessie standing right in front of him?

Fall Fireside (Book 5): Cami Quinn has had enough of being the shiny new date for the cowboys in Quinn Valley. She's on her fifth or sixth broken heart, and she needs the soothing, healing messages she's found at the fall fireside series in the past. Will Cami and Clay find a way to mend what's broken inside themselves in order to find a happily-ever-after?

ABOUT LIZ

Liz Isaacson writes inspirational romance, usually set in Texas, or Wyoming, or anywhere else horses and cowboys exist. She lives in Utah, where she writes full-time, takes her two dogs to the park everyday, and eats a lot of veggies while writing. Find her on her website at feelgoodfictionbooks.com